D0013755

NUMBER ONE ★ GHOST TOWNS ★ MINING CAMPS ★ BODIE, CALIFORNIA

★GHOSTOWNERS★

"Goodbye God, I'm Going to Bodie"

— BY CALAMITY JAN

Calamity Jan

Copyright © 2008
by Jan Pierson

All rights reserved, including the right to
reproduce this book or portions therein
in any form whatsoever.

For information contact:

WildWest Publishing
P O Box 11658
Olympia, WA 98508

Printed in the United States of America
by Gorham Printing, Rochester, Washington
Cover and book design by Kathy Campbell

Fourth WildWest Edition 2008

ISBN13: 978-0-9721800-0-9
ISBN: 0-9721800-0-1
LCCN: 2002107743

http://www.calamityjan.com

Dedicated to

The Friends of Bodie

Bodie State Historic Park

P.O. Box 515

Bridgeport, CA 91517

With special thanks to Bodie Supervising Ranger,
Brad Sturdivant and Ranger Mark and Leona Pupich for their
historical critique, assistance and support.

And finally

My deepest appreciation to Bonnie and Marlene Lewis who took
me over the Sierra Nevada Mountains into this gold mining town
where the little girl who became a legend, captured my heart. The
unknown girl of Bodie who wrote the words GOODBYE GOD, I'M
GOING TO BODIE in her diary over a hundred years ago, will
remind us of children like her, who, despite hardships, quietly
made history and deserve to be remembered.

Bodie, California

Meggie found the diary under a floor board of a crumbling old house that looked as though it had collapsed a hundred years before. A few walls and timbers were left standing like frozen, wind-scarred ghosts.

"Hey, what'd you find?" Paige called out, making her way across the rotting planks and boards toward her best friend.

Meggie Bryson squinted beneath the hot desert sun, staring at the old leather diary she had just pried out of a battered copper tin. Her hands shook with excitement as she gazed at the first entry:

February 13, 1879
Anna Louise Lockmoor
Age 11
Goodbye God, I'm going to Bodie

4

Chapter 1

Meggie drew a deep breath and felt a shiver crawl down her back. "I can't believe this, Paige. You think this is it? You think maybe this is that girl's missing diary—that diary everybody's been looking for?" She struggled to keep her hands steady, her thoughts clear. *Anna Louise Lockmoor, age 11...*

"Like, whoa...!" Paige gazed into Meggie's wide blue eyes, then glanced down at the faded words written over a hundred years before. "And can you believe she was practically our age when she wrote that?"

"I know." Meggie's knuckles whitened as she clung to the thick, leather-bound book.

"It's her, Paige. I'm almost sure this is the girl the park ranger was talking about. The girl who wrote those words in her diary when she came to Bodie—then hid it."

"You're probably right. But why'd she say *that*?" Paige Morefield's eyes were as round as two iron skillets. "Why'd she say goodbye to God?"

Meggie shook her head, her dark blonde hair quivering like desert grass in the wind. "Maybe she was scared." She gazed around at the ghostly shacks and swallowed the big lump caught like sagebrush in her throat. *I'd be scared too, if I had to live in a freaky place like this.*

"Yeah, I'll bet that was it. This was a real bad town, Meggie." Paige inched closer. "Remember the sign when we came in? It said that Bodie used to be the wildest mining camp in the West."

Meggie nodded and shivered again in the heat, staring at the old diary that had been so well hidden, so well preserved after all these years. "Yeah, it's hers. I know it's hers. We found it. We found that missing diary." She looked down at the beat-up copper tin that had hidden it all these years, then back at the worn leather book in her hand.

"Maybe she figured God wouldn't be caught dead in a place like this," Paige went on, her brown eyes still huge.

Meggie turned to her best friend and nodded, figuring she was probably right.

"Well, it's just a ghost town now." Paige tossed her short, dark bob of hair out of her eyes and grinned. "There's nothing wild or bad about Bodie anymore."

Meggie drew a quick breath, hoping Paige was right. She gazed around at the old shacks encircling them here in the high desert countryside near the California-Nevada border. Some buildings were still standing and others were piled like huge sun-bleached bones on the dry, dusty ground. She felt an odd shiver of excitement. This was going to be one fantastic vacation.

"Maybe it was scary moving here then," Paige broke into her thoughts.

But Meggie didn't hear. Her eye caught movement coming

from an old house just to their left. Heart pounding, she braced her tall, lanky frame against a plank and felt a chill crawl like a snake down her back. A shadow. Something moved from behind that old curtain... The shadow hovered, then disappeared.

"What's wrong?" Paige was in her face.

Meggie stared at the hollow, skull-eyed window. She couldn't speak. She couldn't move.

"Whoa! You look like you've seen a ghost!"

Meggie gasped.

"Yeah, well you do, Meggie. You're white as a sheet." Paige grabbed her arm. "What's wrong, anyway?"

Meggie tried to hold herself steady, tried to keep her voice from trembling like the wind. She was pointing at the window now, pointing at that horrible, quivering curtain. "Paige. Someone...some*thing* behind that curtain...is—is—watching us!"

Paige whirled around and stared at the old wooden structure ready to collapse in the next wind.

"It moved. Tha—that cur—curtain...moved," Meggie went on, her words still caught like sagebrush in her throat.

"Wait a minute, Meggie!" Paige threw her hands up in the air and frowned. "Wait a minute..."

Meggie turned and faced her, taking off her glasses slowly.

"You mean that old curtain? That freaky old curtain in the window?"

Meggie nodded, her throat tightening in the hot, smothering breeze.

"Hey, that's only the wind!" Paige laughed, jumping off the

uneven boards and tromping toward the old building next door. Her short hair danced in the breeze. "Meggie Bryson, you've got the wildest imagination in the West. I swear you do." Her words faded as she circled behind the old shack.

"No, Paige, don't!" Meggie yelled, still clinging to the diary. "We don't know that! You didn't see what I saw!" Eyes wide, she called out again, trying to get her glasses back on straight. "It wasn't the wind! Paige! Paige!"

But Paige hadn't heard. She had already entered the back of the dwelling through an old door hanging by one hinge.

"There was a shadow!" Meggie cried, racing toward Paige who had disappeared into the blackness. "Don't go in there! Don't!" Meggie braced herself against the splintery frame, listening to the old door creak and moan in the wind. "Paige! Come out! I—I saw a shadow— behind the curtain...." Her words quivered, then fell in the dust at her feet.

There was no sound except for the creaking door and the empty, hollow blackness that had swallowed up her best friend.

Meggie gripped the diary tighter. No, Paige! *No!* she screamed silently. Why do you have to be so brave all the time? *So stupid.*

And why did she—Meggie Bryson—have to be The Queen of Cowards. Chicken Big. The Ghost Town Wimp?

"Oh Paige—please come out. Please. I don't want to go in there. I can't!"

Suddenly, Meggie heard the boards creak. She saw a shadow in the darkness beyond. It was coming closer.

Closer.

Chapter 2

It was Paige. Meggie almost fainted with joy.

Her best friend stood there, dusting off cobwebs and gunk like it was spaghetti and meatballs from the lunch line at school. "Are you sure you saw something, Meggie?"

Meggie nodded weakly. How could she do this? How could Paige walk smack into that creepy place without so much as blinking an eye?

"Well, I didn't see a thing," Paige muttered. "Except I guess it was sorta dark. Actually, it was as black as a slimeball in there, Meggie. Here, let me show you," she turned and motioned Meggie back into the old shack.

Meggie cringed and backed away from the doorway, backed away from the blackness that could have swallowed up her best friend forever. "Paige, you could have just won the Weiner-Brain-of-the-West contest, hands down. This old dump might be haunted. You didn't see what I did."

"Yeah?" Paige paused and gazed back into the blackness beyond the old door. "You actually think somebody might be following us?"

"That is exactly what I think. But— maybe it's not a—a *person*," she tried not to choke on the words. The freaky door still creaked in the wind.

"Not a person? Hey, wait a minute, Meggie. If that shadow wasn't a person, then..."

Whirling around, Meggie called over her shoulder. "Yeah, Paige. You got it!" *Gee.*

"You mean a ghost?" Paige caught up to Meggie who had jumped up onto the floorboards of the house next door where they'd found the diary just minutes before. Meggie crouched beneath the fallen roof-awning.

"Naw, it couldn't be a ghost, Meggie. Your aunt's been hanging out in ghost towns for years and she says she's never seen a ghost yet. Besides, if Aunt Abby knew Bodie was dangerous, she'd never, ever bring us here. And she did. Hey, we're on this cool little ghost town vacation with your archaeologist aunt, remember? She digs for artifacts and we hang loose and explore. Come on, Meggie…"

"Paige, I'm telling you, I saw something." Meggie wished her heart would quit thumping so loud. She wished she could just explain why it couldn't be the wind.

"I can see why that girl might not've wanted to come here, though," Paige went on, shading her eyes from the sun and staring at some buildings on the eastern slope of the Bodie bluff. "Look at that creepy old mine over there. Maybe ghosts and stuff used to come out of the mine shafts whenever there was a full moon."

Meggie braced herself against a timber and peered between

the rotting planks and shingles. She still couldn't take her eyes off that freaky window next door.

"You know what I think, Meggie?"

"No, what?" she said, slipping on her sunglasses.

"I think we're gettin' carried away. In fact, if you ask me, living in Bodie was probably a blast," Paige tossed back her head and grinned.

Meggie forced her thoughts away from the shadow and turned to her best friend.

"And I'll bet this was her house, Meggie. I'll bet this old pile of boards and bed springs and stuff was where Anna Louise Lockmoor lived."

Meggie drew a deep breath and glanced down at the diary in her sweaty hands. Paige was probably right. She'd been letting her wild imagination get the best of her again. It was dumb. Stupid. They had found a diary, not a ghost.

"Just think about it," Paige went on. "Wouldn't it be cool if you could ride your horse or maybe a stagecoach to school every day? And chase bats and ghosts after dinner instead of unloading the stupid dishwasher?"

Meggie grinned. Paige had a point.

"Wait a sec. There probably weren't any ghosts in Bodie then," Paige rattled on. "A place doesn't even turn into a ghost town until the people leave and that doesn't happen until the gold is gone. And..." she said, fingering her small, firm chin thoughtfully, "if there were any ghosts left hanging around, I'll bet the park rangers scared 'em off."

Meggie hoped Paige was right. Maybe it was just the wind

making that curtain move. Maybe the shadow wasn't anything at all. The park rangers were taking pretty good care of this place. The brochure they handed out at the gate said the California State Parks were keeping it in a state of 'arrested decay,' whatever that meant.

Meggie held the diary close, still sensing they had just made a very important discovery.

"Wait a minute," Paige said, interrupting her thoughts. "What if we're not supposed to keep it."

"Not keep it?" Her grip tightened around the leather book, feeling the sharp brass lacework against her fingers.

"The diary."

"Why not?" Meggie's words felt as sharp-edged as the brass, as tight as her grip.

"Remember what the ranger said?" Paige reminded her. "This is a State Park and we have to leave everything where we found it. We're not supposed to touch anything, Meggie. Not even a tin can. Nothing. And if we find something, we have to report it."

Meggie sighed and rolled her eyes heavenward. Why did Paige have to remember the exact words of the ranger's talk all of a sudden?

"It did practically jump up through the floor boards into our hands, though, didn't it?" Paige went on, the faint trace of a grin curling her lip.

Meggie grinned back, knowing that wasn't exactly how it happened. Actually, the diary had been so well hidden down under the floor boards, they had almost missed it. At first, the old copper tin looked like just another piece of junk. But ghost town detectives don't ignore anything—not even rusty old tins like the one hiding this diary. She drew the book closer, feeling her heart pound against the black leather and darkened brass.

"We need to find out why Anna had to say goodbye to God," Paige told her. "Maybe there was something she knew that we don't. Maybe there was something real dangerous in Bodie. Or someone."

Meggie blinked from behind her wire-framed sunglasses. "Some—one?" Her tall, slender frame grew rigid, her shirt shivered in the wind.

"Remember The Badman From Bodie?" Paige stepped across the floor boards and fallen timbers, then jumped down into the yard strewn with junk and rotting lumber.

Meggie's mind backed up, recalling the legend of this real bad guy who swore all the time, except when he was drawing his gun and shooting somebody. Okay, yeah. The ranger said that back in the 1800's, he was supposed to be the meanest man alive. "But that was over a hundred years ago, Paige." She steadied herself against a plank and glanced back at the old curtain quivering in the window.

"I'M CHIEF OF MURDERTOWN AND I'M DRY!" Paige spit out the words like she'd just bolted out of a saloon and was ready to attack the town single-handed. "WHOSE TREAT IS IT? DON'T ALL SPEAK AT ONCE OR I'LL TURN LOOSE AND SCATTER DEATH AND DESTRUCTION FULL BENT FOR THE NEXT ELECTION!" Her Nikes skidded in the dust, making her look like an outlaw in cutoffs.

"Shh!" Meggie choked, gazing around and hoping nobody heard.

"That's what he said, Meggie! The ranger told us that guy yelled those exact words every time he walked into a saloon or livery stable or hotel." Paige still looked like a sawed-off outlaw on the rampage.

Meggie drew a deep breath and stared at her friend. Part of her wanted to laugh, but the other part knew this wasn't funny. "You think there really was a guy like that living in Bodie?"

"I'm not sure," Paige replied, brown eyes flashing, "but if it was true and Anna knew about him, then no wonder she didn't want to come here." Paige dusted off her cutoffs with slim, sun-browned arms.

It made sense, Meggie realized. The ranger told them there used to be a lot of bad stuff going on around here during the gold mining days. "And maybe there still is..."

"Huh?" Paige paused, and faced her.

"Bad stuff. Bad things happening in Bodie..."

"Yeah, I guess there were robberies and holdups and street fights and a murder every day. Can you believe that, Meggie? A murder in Bodie every day!"

Meggie felt a chill, even under the hot Bodie sun.

"And can you believe that firehouse bell rang every time they buried somebody?" Paige went on, pointing at the old wooden structure with the bell tower in the distance. "I guess people always knew who'd just died or been killed by the number of times it rang. Remember Meggie? One bong for every year. The ranger said that babies and little kids died all the time, too. Sometimes the bell just went on and on..."

"I don't like hearing things like that."

"I don't either," Paige agreed.

"But I want to find out, Paige. I want to read this diary and find out more about what happened to Anna." Meggie gripped the diary tighter. "And," she went on carefully, hoping she could get the words out right, "And..."

"And what?"

Meggie caught her breath and faced Paige. "Okay, we might as well find out if he is still hanging around this place." There. She'd said it.

"Who?"

"The Badman. The Badman From Bodie." Their eyes locked. "In case you forgot, you're the one who brought this up."

"But what if it's just a legend, Meggie? Besides, if he was real, he's gone now, don't you think? Like this town. It's falling apart. It's dead." Her short frame stood tall as she rammed her hands into the back pockets of her cutoffs and threw up her chin.

"I don't care. We need to know." Meggie still couldn't stop thinking about the shadow behind the curtain, wondering if it might have been him. The Badman. But could somebody like that still be hanging around even after—like a hundred years? she wondered. Meggie felt her skin prickle.

"I'll bet the diary's going to tell us, Paige. I'll bet anything we're gonna find out what happened to that girl and what happened here in Bodie." Meggie stepped across the planks and jumped onto the dusty ground strewn with planks and junk, hugging the little black book close. "I can't wait to get back to camp and read what Anna Louise Lockmoor has to say."

"Hey, wait. We can't just walk off with it, can we Meggie?"

"Excuse me?" Meggie gritted her teeth and gripped the book tighter.

"We have to leave stuff where we found it. Remember what the ranger said?"

Meggie knew what the ranger said. She knew exactly what the ranger said. And the park brochure.

"Hey, those are the rules…"

Meggie hesitated, then sighed. "Okay, okay—then we'll put it back under the floor boards and turn it in when we leave Bodie. So, it'll be our secret, Paige. We've got four days left. We can come and read it every day until we have to leave. We have to find out more about Anna." Meggie's faded t-shirt rippled in the wind but her sneakers stood firm.

"Sure. Okay," Paige glanced over her shoulder at the late afternoon sun dropping below California's Eastern Sierras. "Okay, Meggie. It's our secret."

Meggie stood beside her best friend and nodded, casting one last glance at the eerie window with the ragged, shivering curtain. A cold sweat crawled down her neck, making a small, winding trail down her dusty back as it disappeared below her long, straight hair.

Why? Meggie wondered. Why did Anna Louise Lockmoor have to say goodbye to God?

Chapter 3

August 12, 1879

Sometimes I feel so frightened living here in Bodie. There are shootings and robberies and stage holdups almost every day. More and more people keep coming in from Gold Hill and Virginia City. Stage coaches and buckboards and prairie schooners are jest crowding the streets! The hotels and even Blasdell's boarding house are nearly burst at the seams. Opium dens and unsavory people are just everywhere and Mama has to walk me to school because even the good side of town is dangerous. If only we could go back to Ohio! But Mama says no. She says Papa has to work in the mines. And that scares me too. There are so many bad accidents at the Standard Mine. I jest hate listening to the firehouse bell toll every time they bury somebody. I never was so much frightened in my life when I heard that wretched bell for the first time! Everything stops when there's an accident. The mine closes down. The Stamp Mill stops stamping. The saloons go all quiet. People on the streets stop walking with a foot in midair almost. That's the only time it's

quiet around here. Yesterday it rang thirty-seven times
when they buried Jeremy Stevenson's papa.

Meggie felt her throat tighten, then set the diary down. They had come back to the battered remains of the old house first thing the next morning and couldn't stop reading. "Paige, I swear, this is even more unbelievable than Nancy Drew."

Paige nodded in complete agreement.

Meggie was glad they had got an early start. Aunt Abby had dropped them off as soon as the park rangers opened the gate. Meggie was thankful her aunt was busy on her archaeological project, because that meant she and Paige were going to have a lot of freedom. All Aunt Abby could think about was getting up to the Red Cloud Mine which meant she and Paige were probably going to have these next few days to do just about anything they wanted.

Once Aunt Abby got her permit to dig in one hand, and her map and supplies in her nylon backpack in the other, she was off. Meggie realized that she and Paige were going to have so much freedom it might be dangerous, but she wasn't about to complain. She had a feeling these ghost town vacations were just the beginning. It was like she and Paige were standing on the edge of a deep, dark mine; two brand new ghost town detectives ready to jump headlong into danger. Excitement. Mystery.

And maybe Bodie is going to be the most exciting—and the most dangerous ghost town of all, she realized. Meggie glanced down at the diary in her hands, then across the dusty terrain with the fallen bones of a town that had finally died. "I feel sorry for that girl, though, don't you, Paige? I mean, this was probably a terrible place to live."

"Yeah. And I guess Anna doesn't get to ride a horse or a stagecoach to school, huh? It looks like walking to school was even more dangerous than sledding down Schmid's Hill or jumping off the Trout Creek bridge."

Meggie gripped the diary tighter and swallowed the huge lump that was stuck like a rock in her throat.

"Let's read more," Paige went on, taking the diary from Meggie and turning a page. "The ranger was right, though. This place must've been pretty wild."

Suddenly Meggie heard footsteps coming through the sagebrush. She gave Paige a quick warning jab with her elbow, then squinted through the cracks of the fallen roof. She drew a sharp breath, then sighed with relief. It was the park ranger who had given the history talk the day before. Paige had already slipped the diary back down under the floor boards. *Yesss. Cool move, Paige.*

"Hi," Meggie called, getting up and absently brushing some dust from her cutoffs.

"Hi," the ranger called back. "You two having fun here in Bodie?"

"Uh, yes. Definitely," Paige spoke up. "Your talk was really, *really* interesting yesterday."

The soft grey-green eyes crinkled as the striking young ranger smiled and paused. "This was a fascinating town," she told them, adjusting her straw Stetson hat on her mass of strawberry-blonde curls. Her khaki short-sleeved shirt and dark green slacks blended with the dry, earth-colored tones around them.

"Did you know that these buildings are only a fraction of

what was once here?" She gestured, pointing to the sagebrush-covered hillside dotted with the sparse dwellings left standing. "On the eastern slope of Bodie Bluff you can still see the remains of the Standard Mine and Mill, though. That mine produced nearly fifteen million dollars and was the reason for the 1878 rush to Bodie. At one time there were thirty mines operating at once—all of them bringing in more than a hundred million dollars before Bodie turned into a ghost."

A ghost? Meggie almost choked.

"A hundred million dollars?" Paige threw her hands on her hips and shook her head, her short bob of hair dancing like a buckboard canvas. "Whoa! That is a lot of money!"

"Between 1877 and 1881 more than ten-thousand people lived here," the ranger went on. "Those were the boom years."

Meggie's thoughts backed up. *That's when Anna was here...*

"Unfortunately, in 1932 a fire destroyed about two-thirds of this town. You girls happen to be standing on the edge of the 'respectable' section," she went on. "Over there beyond the jailhouse was the bad side of town. Gambling halls, opium dens, and a lot more went on during those years. Can you believe there were once sixty-five saloons in Bodie?"

"Whoa again!" Paige almost fell over. "They must've been pretty thirsty when they came out of the mines."

Meggie smothered a grin.

"Did The Badman From Bodie live in that part of town?" Paige asked, casting a sidelong glance at Meggie.

"There were a lot of bad men in Bodie. That was a common phrase and some people believe the term just meant you were a rough character. By the way," she smiled, reaching out her hand, "I'm Ranger Downing. I believe I've met your aunt. She's the consulting archaeologist looking for some artifacts at the Red Cloud Mine, isn't she?"

"Yup, that's our Aunt Abby. She's actually Meggie's aunt, though," Paige replied, pumping the young ranger's hand. "But she's going to be taking me to the ghost towns, too. That way Meggie won't get bored. This is our first ghost town actually."

"Paige"... Meggie rolled her eyes, then turned to the ranger. "I'm Meggie and this is Paige," she said, shaking her hand.

"Aren't you camping down along the Walker River?" Ranger Downing asked.

Paige nodded. "The Flat Shingle Mill Campground."

"Shingle Mill Flat Campground," Meggie corrected.

"What's the difference?" Paige went on with a shrug. "Anyway, it's really fun up here. Ghost towns are SO cool. We're probably going to be archaeologists when we grow up, except I might be a pilot or a waitress."

Ranger Downing smiled and took off her hat, fanning herself from the heat. "Where are you girls from?" she asked.

"Trout Lake," Meggie told her.

"Trout Lake?"

"It's in Washington State," Paige put in. "Right after you cross the bridge from Oregon into Washington, you cut up at the mouth of the White Salmon River and go through Husum. Trout Lake is only eleven miles past BZ Corners."

"BZ Corners? Oh..."

Meggie could see the ranger wasn't getting it. "You cross the

Columbia River at Hood River on the Hood River Bridge," she explained. "Paige also forgot to mention the town of White Salmon which is on the Washington side. Most people get confused if we leave out White Salmon."

"Yeah," Paige agreed. "BZ Corners usually throws everybody off too."

"Trout Lake is right near Mt. Adams," Meggie went on. "You can't miss it."

"Mt. Adams?"

Meggie nodded, surprised she didn't know about Mt. Adams either. "It's the second tallest mountain in our state," she told Ranger Downing, "in fact I'll bet it's even higher than where we're standing right now." Meggie knew the elevation was over eight thousand feet right here in the Sierra Nevada mountains—right here in Bodie.

"No I didn't realize..." Ranger Downing didn't seem quite as confused now.

"You'd like living in Trout Lake," Paige told her. "There's a lot to do. Probably even more stuff going on in Trout Lake than in New York or BZ Corners."

Meggie frowned. "Paige..."

Ranger Downing smiled. "I'm sure I'd like it," she said, and Meggie could see that she meant it. "Well, there's a lot to do and see here in Bodie too, and if you have any questions, be sure to look me up. If you can't find me walking around, I'll probably be at the park office on Green Street or in the Museum. The Museum is on Main Street, just beyond the morgue."

The morgue? Meggie cringed.

"Bye, Ranger Downing. And thanks for telling us more about Bodie," Paige called out, waving.

As soon as the ranger was out of sight, Paige pulled the diary back out of its hiding place. "She's nice, isn't she? If we have to give this thing up before we leave, let's make sure we give it to her," Paige said.

Meggie agreed, her thoughts shifting. "I didn't know you wanted to be a waitress, Paige."

"It's a possibility. That way I could eat french fries all day if I wanted. Or pizza."

Meggie looked down into her best friend's face. Even though they were both twelve, Paige was a lot shorter.

"Mom practically forces me to eat vegetables, Meggie. It's disgusting."

"Yeah. I know the feeling. If my little brother and sisters and I don't clean up our plates after dinner, we don't get to watch TV or do anything fun. Can you believe I got grounded for putting some broccoli in my slouch socks? I hate broccoli, Paige, and my folks practically force me to eat it. The last time I got grounded I couldn't even use the phone for two days."

"I don't think parents should be so hard on kids."

Meggie agreed one-hundred percent. "I'll bet it would've been a lot more fun living in the olden days, don't you?"

"Definitely," Paige replied, taking the diary from Meggie's hands and reading the entry dated September 16, 1879.

Today is the first Monday of the month which means I'll be helping Mama with the wash. I don't mind pumping and fetching the water, though. I don't even mind scrubbing

23

Papa's soiled clothes on that washboard! Fact is, I think all this working and scrubbing helps keep me warm, and that's good since I've been having these wretched chills lately. I declare, the drafts coming through these cracks in the walls make me shiver right down to my wool leggings. Winter is almost here and folks say it can get frightfully cold in Bodie. I hear that sometimes it drops nigh to thirty degrees below zero. Mary Beth Cooley says that the snow can get so deep, one can scarcely get through the drifts to find the outhouse! She told me that even the winds creep through the cracks in the houses and snuff out the lanterns. But I shant fret about such dismul things. Tonight Mama's letting me fix potatoes for dinner. I'm going to save some of mine and put them in Papa's lunch pail for a treat. Won't he be surprised! Mama said that if I keep helping her like this, she'll buy some seeds at the Boone Store and let me plant some vegetables and flowers in the spring. Beans and turnips and perhaps some corn. And oh, yes—daisies. Some white daisies. Imagin! My very own garden. I must stop complaining. I know I must be luckier than most children.

Anna's house?

Chapter 4

Meggie and Paige stared at the words, then closed the diary. Except for a few coyotes howling in the distance, it was quiet. Dead quiet.

Meggie felt like some sagebrush and rocks were stuck in her throat, but it was only a lump. A big one.

"Can't they turn up the heat, Meggie?" Paige said finally. "She's getting cold and it isn't even winter."

Meggie couldn't answer. The words had backed up in her throat, feeling cold and thick like the ice and snow that must have crept through Anna's house winter after winter after winter.

"Meggie?"

"Uh—I guess so. I mean no. Wait a minute, Paige..." Meggie frowned.

"Yeah?"

"How could they turn up the heat? They didn't have furnaces. Or wall heaters you just plug in."

"Probably no hair dryers either. Especially if they don't even have a bathroom inside the house."

Meggie agreed.

"And can you believe she's happy helping her mother with the wash, Meggie? Happy."

No. It was hard to believe. "I get upset when Mom asks me to wash my jeans or do my laundry in the automatic washing machine. Or when I have to unload and fold clothes from the dryer."

"What's a washboard?" Paige went on, frowning.

"I don't think it's much like our Maytag," she replied, figuring washboards probably didn't have 'Gentle' 'Regular' and 'Heavy' cycle buttons, either.

"Probably not."

"Uh, why don't we check out the Museum?" Meggie said finally, wishing she could swallow the stupid lump that kept getting stuck in her throat every time they read the diary. This wasn't quite as exciting as Nancy Drew anymore, yet part of her didn't want to stop reading.

"Sure—okay," Paige said with a shrug. "Besides, if we hang out around here too long, somebody might get suspicious." Paige's eyes were wide, almost glassy, which told Meggie she probably needed a break too.

After they put the diary back in its hiding place, they headed back to the center of Bodie where the tourists were milling around. Meggie and Paige walked along the boardwalk past the Boone Store and Warehouse, then crossed the intersection. The morgue stood on the corner like a square brown skull with glassy window-eyes.

Meggie grimaced, then hurried past to the Museum next door.

"Wait a minute!" Paige called out, motioning Meggie back to the window in the front. "There's caskets and stuff lying all over the place. It's really freaky."

But Meggie wasn't interested. Cemeteries and morgues were even more depressing than eating broccoli. But when she got inside the Museum, two big old hearses in the back almost jumped out at her. They looked like two huge iron spiders with caskets on top. She cringed and drew back.

"Hey, cool!" Paige said, walking inside and staring at the funeral display in the far back.

Meggie wasn't impressed. She turned to leave, and then something on the right caught her eye. Walking over to an old display case, she gazed down at a picture under the glass—a picture of a girl about her age. Her pulse quickened. *Was it her?* Meggie inched closer. The girl had long, dark curls and was carrying some daisies. She was so pretty it almost took Meggie's breath away.

"Whoa, is that Anna?" Paige asked, coming up from behind and peering over Meggie's shoulder.

Meggie couldn't answer, but she knew. "Yes. It's her. I'm almost positive it's Anna." Her knuckles whitened as she leaned closer and stared at the small photograph under the glass.

"Let's ask." Paige whirled around and headed toward the main desk where some park rangers were answering questions and giving out brochures.

But the ranger in charge said he didn't know. "Just a little girl from Bodie," he told them. "Long forgotten, I suppose."

"The daisies…" Meggie said the minute they were outside.

"In the picture she was holding some daisies, Paige." Meggie's throat felt tight, her words stiff. "Remember in the diary? She wanted to plant some daisies in the spring."

"I'll bet anything it's her!" Paige grabbed her arm. "Anything!"

Meggie agreed, trying to hold back the excitement racing through her veins. "Maybe the diary is going to tell us more. Give us more clues. Let's go back to Anna's house, Paige. I think we have to read more. Oh, wow—whether we like it or not, I think Anna Louise Lockmoor has a lot more to tell us." She brushed a blond straggle of hair from her face. "A lot."

They held each others' gaze. They both knew what they had to do.

Meggie and her best friend crossed the intersection, slowing down in front of the Boone Store and Warehouse where Anna's mother probably bought her those seeds. The store was empty now. She and Paige paused and looked in the windows at the dusty old shelves and counters where Anna and her parents must have purchased potatoes and seeds and the things they needed. Peeling wallpaper hung down like hungry tongues hankering for food. But there was nothing left but empty pickle barrels and crates and rotting sacks which once held flour or sugar or grain. Meggie glanced at Paige, then backed away.

Up the street, Ranger Downing was giving another history talk to a large group of tourists in front of the old Methodist church. She waved her Stetson and motioned them over.

"Let's see if she has any more important stuff to tell us about

28

Bodie," Paige suggested.

Meggie hesitated. "We need to get back to that diary."

"Come on, Meggie!" Paige called, motioning for her to follow.

Reluctantly, she followed Paige toward the crowd of people scattered around listening to Ranger Downing. "We only have a few days left in Bodie," she whispered, plopping down on the church steps beside her best friend. Meggie hoped this wasn't going to be too historical.

"This church was built in 1882 and is the only church still standing," the ranger said to the crowd. "THE TEN COMMANDMENTS painted on oilcloth and hanging behind the pulpit, was stolen. 'Thou Shalt Not Steal' didn't always apply in Bodie. Two blocks up the street the first schoolhouse was burned down by an early-day juvenile delinquent."

"Even the kids in Bodie were bad," Paige said under her breath.

"Except Anna," Meggie reminded her, fanning herself with a park brochure she had picked up off the ground. Her glasses began to steam up from her sweat, her clothes sticking like damp moss to her skin.

After Ranger Downing finished her talk, Meggie got up and led the way past some old houses and buildings and a small sawmill, all scattered around like bones. But this was the way Meggie wanted to learn about history. Hearing talks and getting stuff out of books at school was okay, but this was even better. Meggie wanted to *feel* the History, to walk on it—to touch the old boards, the dust, the leather diary in her hands...

"Ranger Downing is really cool, isn't she?" Paige said, breaking into her thoughts.

Meggie paused and nodded. "Yeah, I like her a lot. She makes everything seem like it's now instead of yesterday."

"If I decide not to be an archaeologist or a pilot or a waitress, I might be a park ranger," Paige told her, walking on.

Meggie grinned and pulled back her long, straight hair, knotting it. "Mmm, well why not? I guess it might be pretty cool being a park ranger if you could hang out in a ghost town every day."

She walked beside Paige along the rotting boardwalk, her ponytail swinging from side to side. Suddenly she stopped in front of an old house with ragged curtains hanging like shrouds in the window. The curtains trembled from the hot, dry wind creeping through the cracks, reminding her of that freaky old curtain in the house next to where they had found the diary. But that wasn't anything after all, she reminded herself. Paige proved that. The shadow and stuff had only been her imagination. Or the wind. Meggie felt an odd chill and gazed around, listening to a coyote yip-yip-yipping somewhere in the distance. She wrapped her arms around herself and shivered. Sure. Probably just the wind.

"What's wrong?" Paige asked, glancing back.

Meggie caught her breath.

"You look like you just ate some broccoli. Or saw a ghost..."

"Cut it out, Paige." Meggie frowned, wishing she could explain the feeling. But she couldn't. And that stupid coyote wasn't helping either. She forced her uneasy thoughts aside and changed the subject. "We need to keep out of sight, though," she told Paige when they neared the shack where the diary was hidden.

"Why?"

"If somebody sees us hanging around the same place too long, they might wonder if we're hiding something. They might come looking or make us leave."

But Meggie knew that this part of Bodie was off the beaten track. Most of these dwellings had either fallen down or were destroyed by one of the fires. What was left of Anna's house wouldn't be half as interesting as the buildings that still had windows and doors and furniture inside. That's where the tourists hung out. Anna's roof had toppled and was lying sideways like a rotting wooden awning waiting to collapse under the next winter snow pack. For now, though, the roof-awning shaded them from the hot Bodie sun. And it kept them fairly well hidden so that they could read the diary without being seen.

By the time they reached Anna's house, Meggie felt better. She looked around at the shacks and outbuildings surrounding them and realized that if somebody had actually been in that old house next door, Paige might not have come out alive. *And Paige Morefield is about as alive as any twelve-year-old kid I know.* Meggie smiled to herself, retrieving the book from its hiding place beneath the dry, worm-eaten timbers. The wind made the boards and timbers creak and sent the sagebrush crawling like giant spiders past the house. Nobody can see us, and even if they could, who'd care about two girls hanging out in some old shack on the edge of Bodie?

They took turns reading, unaware that the amber sun was

sinking and that it was almost time to meet Aunt Abby in the parking lot.

"Whoa, we forgot to eat lunch," Paige laughed, yanking her sandwich, cookies and soda out of her backpack. She began eating the cookies. "I just love being on our own like this, Meggie. At home Mom would kill me if I ate my dessert first."

Meggie was still stuck like pitch to the diary. "Hey, wait a minute. Look, Paige." she reached absently for a Pepsi. "Will you just look at this..."

November 7, 1879

I have a friend now. His name is Johnny. Johnny Merritt. Most of the children at school shun him because he lives on the bad side of town. They call him an Urchin, but he's not. He doesn't throw rocks at the Chinamen like some of the boys on the good side of town do! He can't help it if he's got holes in his shoes and tattered clothes. I sowed him a fine jacket from some leftover scraps of wool Mama let me have. He was so proud and thankful, he gave me his dough balls. Why, they're the prettiest marbles in Bodie! Johnny and his ma baked and painted them all fancy. I'm putting them in my tin of treasures. I think maybe I love those dough balls even more than my little tea set and porsalin doll. Maybe as much as my locket. Since Bodie is such a frightfully bad place though, I think I'm going to keep my tin of treasures hidden. I found the perfect hiding place yesterday!

Meggie set the diary down and looked at Paige. She didn't know what to say. And the lump was back. The biggest ever.

A pack rat scurried past and sent her pop can flying. "Yeeow!" she exploded, nearly knocking down the wall.

"Hey, it's only a rat, Meggie! What's the big deal? It could'a been a rattlesnake or a black widow spider or a tarantula or..."

"I don't care what it is, I don't want it to sneak up on me!"

"So, what's the big problem?" Paige went on.

Meggie snorted, dusting off her arms.

"A dumb little thing like that doesn't usually freak you out, Meggie. If it was the Badman From Bodie or a poisonous rattlesnake or something like that, maybe I could understand."

"I know. But that was a big rat. A big one," she replied lamely.

Paige paused and glanced down at the diary, then back up into Meggie's face. "There's something else, isn't there?"

Meggie caught Paige's gaze, unblinking.

"What is it, Meggie?"

Meggie drew a deep breath. "Okay. It's her. Anna."

Paige moved closer.

"It's like she's here, Paige. Right here in this old pile of boards that might've been her house. It's like she's been talking to us ever since we came to Bodie and found this diary."

Paige nodded. "I know. I've been feeling that way, too."

"I mean, she's so happy when she gets to haul water and use a washboard and fix potatoes and plant a vegetable garden. That means she probably eats those vegetables, Paige. Like it's a privilege."

Paige nodded again. "And now she's talking about her treasures.

Can you believe they fit in a little tin box? I mean, I've got drawers full of stuff—and boxes in our basement and Grandma's attic, too."

"Yeah, me too. Not even a mega tin box could hold my soccer ball, baseball bat, sixteen Barbies and four Kens—you know, stuff you want to keep forever."

"Mine either. Especially if we include the wardrobes, make-up sets, dressers and sports cars. And CD's an—and..."

"I know. And dough balls. She was so excited about her little dough balls, Paige. And she made her friend a jacket from scraps and everybody was so happy."

"When Mom won't hem my jeans, I get upset."

"They're happy with scraps and I won't be caught dead in my cousin's hand-me-down designer jeans," Meggie rattled on, fingering her ponytail absently. "All this makes me feel so weird, Paige. I don't think I can handle another word in that diary right now."

"Me neither," Paige agreed. "So, let's try to find it."

Meggie drew back "Huh? Find what?"

"Her tin of treasures," Paige replied.

"Her tin of treasures?"

"Yeah, remember? She hid it."

"Hey, whoa! That's right." Meggie gazed straight into Paige's wide brown eyes.

"So, let's see if we can find out where Anna Louise Lockmoor hid her treasures!"

Meggie felt shivers of excitement crawl like centipedes down her neck. Carefully, she slipped the diary back into the tin and down under the floor boards.

...I'm going to keep my tin of treasures hidden. I found the perfect hiding place yesterday.

Bodie Museum

Chapter 5

Meggie and Paige searched and searched Anna's house and the outbuildings for the rest of the afternoon, but they just couldn't find it. Anna had done a good job of hiding her treasures.

"We have to get back," Meggie said finally, glancing at her watch. "We promised we'd meet Aunt Abby at the parking lot by five and I don't want to blow it. She might invite one of my little sisters to the next ghost town instead of me."

"Yeah, but since I don't have any sisters or brothers, I don't have to worry about that. Except she's your aunt and if she doesn't invite you, she probably won't invite me, either. Yeah, let's go, Meggie."

Meggie agreed, following Paige past the old shack. Suddenly, she saw the shadow again. The ragged curtain shivered like a death warning. She stopped short, nearly losing her balance. "Paige..."

Paige turned back and faced her. "Yeah?"

"Ahhh—th—" Meggie pointed at the creepy skull window, her face as pale as the curtain. "Th—the shadow..."

"You are serious?"

Meggie nodded, then took off running, leaving Paige in her dust. The long copper fingers of the late afternoon sun stretched across the desert floor, prodding them on. They skirted sagebrush, weaving around old shacks and debris like jet-propelled gophers, passing the firehouse and the Wells Fargo Express Office, then up the street past the morgue and church.

"Wh—Who do you think it was?" Paige asked as soon as they were back in the parking lot. She braced herself against the restroom, panting.

Meggie shook her head, her ponytail flying. She wished she knew.

"The Badman From Bodie maybe?" Paige went on, wiping the dirt from her small turned-up nose and cheeks with her shirt.

Meggie was still trying to catch her breath. "You heard Ranger Downing. She said that the name probably fit a—a lot of guys back then. Nobody knows. Anyway, whoever he was or they were, they're dead now. That was a hundred years ago, Paige!"

"So what? There was this old guy near BZ Corners who was almost a hundred years old, Meggie. He was a photographer and he used to run all over the place taking pictures. He didn't wear hearing aids or glasses and Mom says he almost ran to the BZ Store to get his newspaper every day."

But before Meggie could answer, her aunt's van pulled into the parking lot.

"Let's go, troops!" Aunt Abby called out, waving her wide-brimmed straw hat. Her face and hair was covered with brown dust. Meggie couldn't even see the gray in her hair now. Her aunt looked younger.

"Have a nice day?" she asked as the old vehicle rattled down the dirt road toward Bridgeport and their campsite beyond.

"Oh yeah, Aunt Abby!" Paige told her, smiling.

"You two look like you just crawled out of a rat hole," she laughed, her baggy plaid shirt flapping in the warm wind coming through the window. "Almost as bad as me!"

Meggie grinned, realizing that even though she was amost fifty years old, her aunt didn't seem old at all. In fact, Aunt Abby was more fun than most kids, and definitely more fun than most adults. Her mom explained that she was still part-Hippie which might account for why she was so cool.

"I hope you're not feeling neglected," she said to the girls.

"Oh no..." they both said a bit too loudly.

"It's just that I've just been involved in such a fascinating dig at the Red Cloud Mine. In fact, I can hardly keep my nose out of the dirt and crannies, I'm afraid. But it's worth it. I'm uncovering some wonderful artifacts for the Bureau of Mines."

"We're having fun too, Aunt Abby," Paige told her.

"Yes," Meggie added carefully, adjusting her sunglasses. "We're learning a lot about Bodie. A lot."

Paige glanced at Meggie and nodded. "Yes. We go to the Museum and listen to the ranger's talks and things like that."

"And when you're not listening to the ranger or aren't in the Museum, you know about the rules, of course. Leave everything as you find it and such," Aunt Abby put in.

"Oh yes, we read that in the brochure," Meggie said with

conviction.

"And Ranger Downing told us the same thing," Paige added with wide, unblinking eyes.

Aunt Abby nodded. "It's hard though, isn't it?"

Meggie drew a deep breath. "Yes. Yes, it is, Aunt Abby."

"Yes, well it would be for me, too," her aunt said to them both. "I don't know what I'd do if I didn't have permission to dig."

Meggie cleared her throat as the van rattled down the gravel road.

"I know you're doing everything in your power to stay with the rules there at Bodie, though—to do the right thing and not disturb things," Aunt Abby went on. "I know you're really working on that."

"Oh, yes," Paige said. "We're definitely working on that."

Meggie nodded in agreement. It was just so cool the way her aunt understood how things were. Maybe it was because her aunt had a whole bunch of college degrees. Being part-Hippie probably helped a lot too. Before long, they pulled into the campground and parked along side the tent.

That night after a supper around the campfire, Meggie and Paige went down by the river to make plans. Aunt Abby worked on some reports by the light of the kerosene lantern. A clean, sage-filled breeze rustled the dry grass as they slid down the bank to the rocks below.

"We need to be more careful now that we know somebody might be following us," Meggie said carefully, watching the water ripple down from the Nevada border. She had already ruled out a ghost, though. Aunt Abby had never seen a ghost in any ghost town she had ever visited so why should Bodie be any different? "But somebody is following us, Paige. I know it."

"If that's true, you don't think they saw us hide the diary before we left, do you?" Paige said to her.

Meggie threw her hand against her head, realizing they probably shouldn't have left it back there. "Oh noo…"

"Well, if the diary is gone when we get back tomorrow, then we'll know, won't we?"

"Gee. We just didn't have time to think. Besides, we had to follow those rules." Meggie forced her thoughts away from the depressing possibility and began to make plans for the following day. By the time they returned to the campsite, Aunt Abby had already turned in for the night. Meggie peeked into the van and saw that she was asleep.

Tired, she and Paige crawled into the tent and turned out the lantern, listening to the coyotes howl in the distant hills beyond. Clouds scudded past the bright moon while nightfall covered the small tent with its dark blanket.

Thankfully, when they got back to Bodie the next morning, they discovered the diary was exactly where they had left it. Relief flooded Meggie's senses. She held the diary close as though it was a long-lost friend.

"She has a lot more to tell us, Paige. We're getting close, I just feel it." Meggie felt so much better knowing that if somebody had been watching them, this diary wouldn't even be here.

"I hope you're right," Paige replied, stepping over the rusted remains of an old wood stove. She paused and stooped over, opening what appeared to be the oven door. "Nope, not in here either..."

Meggie read the diary while Paige searched for the tin of treasures, both keeping one eye open for any sign of movement. Except for a few rabbits and blue birds darting overhead, there was nothing—nothing except the quiet creaking and rattling of boards in the dry desert wind or the thump of timber and metal as Paige rummaged through every inch of the house and out-buildings. The only building they hadn't explored thoroughly was the one with the creepy curtains shivering like grave-clothes in the window. Even though Meggie knew there was nothing to worry about, she still kept her distance. Besides, Paige had already checked it out.

Meggie read on, searching for some clue that might tell them where Anna had hidden her treasures. But the little girl from Bodie didn't say another word about her special box. "It's like she's got this secret and nobody but Johnny Merritt is going to know what it is," Meggie told Paige, wiping the sweat from her face.

Overhead the sun told them it was about noon. Taking a break, Meggie slipped the diary back in its hiding place.

"I can't find a thing, Meggie," Paige said, looking like she had just crawled out of a garbage can. She plopped down on the boards beside Meggie and rummaged through her pack, pulling out a banana. "Nothing. Maybe Anna buried her tin of trea-sures. Or maybe she took them with her when she left Bodie."

"But if she left Bodie, why didn't she take her diary too?" Meggie reached for a sandwich and took a bite. "If Anna hid one, wouldn't she hide the other?"

Paige shook her head as she peeled her banana.

Then Meggie caught her breath, nearly choking on her sandwich. There it was again. The shadow disappeared behind the old house with the ghost curtains. *Somebody is following us.* Her flesh crawled as she groped for Paige's arm and squeezed it slowly.

Paige dropped her banana. She got the message.

Meggie sat unmoving, her eyes sliding sideways from behind her glasses. But it was gone. As quickly as she had seen the shadow, it disappeared, crawling like a snake behind the skeleton shacks.

She tried to speak but her words felt as thick as the dry dust encircling them. So it wasn't her wild imagination after all. "Uh, w—we are def—definitely being followed," she said through tight lips.

Paige slapped a fly on the frayed edge of her cutoffs.

Meggie caught her breath and turned to Paige, wondering if she had heard. "Paige, I—I said we're being followed."

"Whaat?"

"I said, we're being followed, Paige! Didn't you see that shadow?"

Paige rolled her eyes heavenward. "We know it's not a ghost and if it's The Badman From Bodie, he's too old to run us down." She picked up the banana she had dropped and started picking off the splinters and dirt.

"Paige, that's stupid. Put down that dumb banana. We're being followed and it isn't The Badman From Bodie."

"Yeah, yeah, okay. But are you absolutely positive you saw

somebody?" She stuffed the banana in her mouth.

"Of course I saw somebody," Meggie sputtered, pointing toward the house and outbuildings to her left. "A shadow. It just slid around the corner of that old shack like...like..."

"It's not a ghost, Meggie. Aunt Abby says there aren't any in ghost towns, but just in case she's wrong about Bodie, the rangers probably scared 'em off, remember?"

"We don't know that for sure..."

"Well, whoever it was, he's gone now." Paige munched the banana and retrieved the diary.

Meggie drew a deep breath and gazed around, then looked at her half-pint friend eating the banana like she was Tarzan and Meggie was Jane. How could she be so laid back when danger lurked around every shack and bush? Meggie wondered. But the coast was clear. It was safe now, wasn't it? Whoever-it-was had vanished—like a—a ghost. She almost choked on the word.

"Hey, Meggie—look at this!"

Meggie forced down her sandwich and sat down beside Paige. Adjusting her glasses, she read the entry dated February 29, 1880:

It's been so cold. The winds howl like terrible wolves and the freezing air sneaks through every nook and cranny. We can nary keep the house warm enough with the cook stove and scant wood we find. Sometimes the snow is piled so high we can scarcely open our door one single crack. I'm sure Papa isn't telling Mama and me how bad things are. And he and Mama insist I have the wool quilt to keep warm. But I

43

still shiver, even with the quilt and scratchy woolens piled ever so high. Lately, I don't even have the strength to help with the chores. Poor Mama. Sometimes I'm jest heartbroke watching her do the chores by herself now. And I don't get to school much anymore, either. Or to church on Sundays on account of I'm having such frightful bad chills and coughing spells. Mama looks so worried but I tell her and Papa I'm feeling considerable better than I really am. Spring is coming and I must gather my strength to plant my garden.

Abandoned house

Chapter 6

"You're both so quiet tonight," Aunt Abby said after they had finished dinner and were sitting together around the campfire toasting marshmallows on a stick. "Is anything wrong? Aren't you having a good time exploring Bodie?"

Paige sat up straight and forced a wide smile. "Oh yeah. We are. This is probably the most exciting ghost town we've ever, ever visited. Ever." She wiped some marshmallow off her mouth, the smile still stuck to her face.

Meggie agreed. It was the truth. Everything, that was, except the the part about Anna. Reading about Anna getting cold and sick wasn't exciting at all.

"Well I'm glad you're enjoying yourselves," Aunt Abby went on. "I don't know if you know it or not, but even though just a fraction of the original town is still standing, Bodie is still one of the country's largest and best-preserved ghost towns. Did you girls realize that the mines produced millions of dollars worth of gold and silver before they played out?"

Paige nodded. "The ranger told us a lot of stuff like that."

"The Standard Mine and Stamp Mill was the biggest

producer and the lucky break came when it caved in in the mid-1870's and exposed a much richer pocket of gold ore than they'd ever seen. Miners began earning almost $900 per day."

Meggie drew back in surprise. $900 a day? Whoa. Maybe Anna's Papa got rich. Maybe they could afford to leave Bodie. Maybe Anna got away. Meggie's thoughts raced, her hopes rose.

"You sure know a lot about Bodie, don't you?" Paige put in, pulling her marshmallow and stick out of the fire and blowing out the flames.

Aunt Abby smiled and got up, tossing the last of the paper plates into the fire. "I study every ghost town we visit, especially when I'm on an assignment. It's fascinating learning the history of these places, these people."

Meggie was beginning to agree with her one-hundred percent. Especially since they'd met Anna. She sucked the last golden-brown marshmallow off her stick and got up.

"What's a Stamp Mill, Aunt Abby?" Paige asked. "I keep hearing about the Standard Stamp Mill and I know they probably weren't making postage stamps, right?"

Aunt Abby smiled. "Right, Paige. The Stamp Mill was the part of the mining operation where the machinery pounded out the rock, crushing it and separating it from the gold and silver ore. It took fourteen men to operate Standard's twenty stamp mill. Twenty stamp machines were pounding out that ore.

"The mill burned down in 1899, though," she went on, "and even though it was rebuilt and went on functioning after that, it never produced like it had before. It finally shut down in the

1930's and by World War I, only about 100 people were left in Bodie. By the 1940's, almost everybody was gone. The California State Parks took it over in 1962."

Meggie wondered how old Anna might have been when the last person left Bodie. Or did she stay that long? Maybe she and her parents got rich and left Bodie, but if she had stayed, wouldn't she have been in her sixties when the last people left? Maybe she was a Grandma by then and gave her treasures to her grandchildren. Meggie smiled to herself. That was a nice thought.

Meggie wanted to find out more about what happened to Anna, but now that they knew they were being followed, she felt uneasy. Who was following them? she wondered. Who—or what could have disappeared into thin air like that? Meggie felt an odd chill, forcing the ghost thoughts away from her mind.

"There aren't any ghosts in ghost towns, are there?" Paige's words jarred Meggie.

"Why, no, Paige," Aunt Abby replied. "At least not as long as I've been banging around the western United States. No. No ghosts. Nothing but a few lizards and rats and maybe some bats in the mine shafts," she said with a smile, placing her laptop computer on the picnic table beside some research papers.

Meggie caught Paige's gaze, then looked away. Just because Aunt Abby never saw a ghost didn't mean there weren't any. If that had been a *person* following them, it couldn't have disappeared into thin air. And that's what happened. That's exactly what happened. No. Meggie wasn't convinced. She wasn't convinced at all. She opened her Anne Of Green Gables book and tried to concentrate on the story, but it wasn't half as interesting as the Anna she and Paige had been reading about. Meggie could hardly wait to get back to the diary. Yet part of her felt scared, too. Not just for them, but for Anna Louise Lockmoor. Was she going to get better? Was she going to make it through the winter so that she could plant her garden in the spring? Meggie tried to keep her mind on Anne of Green Gables, but the Anna from Bodie kept creeping back.

When they returned to Anna's house the next day, she and Paige circled the house and outbuildings and ruins, but there was no sign of anyone. No footprints. Nothing. Meggie gazed around on the quiet desert landscape and felt a strange, cold foreboding. But a ghost doesn't leave footprints, she said silently, her t-shirt quivering in the morning wind. She reached under the floorboards and retrieved the tin. Even though Meggie knew someone or some*thing* might be watching them, they had to get that diary and finish reading. If her treasures were still here, they had to find them. Time was running out. After today, they had just one more day left to explore Bodie.

The noon sun beat hot against the fallen timbers when Meggie came to the entry dated July 30, 1880. Paige handed her some food, but Meggie wasn't hungry. She could hardly stop reading.

Oh, my garden is so beautiful! Especially my daisies. Except for some sagebrush and wild iris, there was nary a thing growing when we came to Bodie. With such freezes (even in June!) folks said it couldn't be done. But now my vegetables are peeping up with little green noses and fluffy bonnets. Mama insists I have my picture taken with a bokay of my daisies. She even made me a new muslin dress for the occasion. Oh, I'm so glad I don't have to wear my tiresome, scratchy wool frock another day! It did help to keep me warm during the terrible winter, though. I'm coughing less and do think I'm feeling considerable better now that the snow is gone and the sun is shining big and round and warm. Mama lets me play with Johnny if we don't stray too far. Johnny is such a special friend. I feel so happy and safe when I'm with him. Sometimes when we tire of exploring or playing marbles, we fetch wood or he helps me weed and haul water for my garden. I give him carrots for a treat and oh, you should see him smile!

Meggie turned to Paige who had just finished her sandwich and was staring at her Snickers bar in one hand and her package of M&M's in the other.

"I wonder about those daisies, Paige..."

"I'm still thinking about the carrots. That was their treat, Meggie. Carrots were treats." Paige kept staring at her candy.

But Meggie's thoughts still lingered on the daisies. "Remember the picture in the Museum?"

Paige stuffed the candy back in her sack like they were chocolate covered snakes and candy-covered snake eggs, then looked up. "What'd you say?"

"In the Museum. She was holding those daisies in the picture, remember? It almost proves she was Anna."

49

Paige nodded. "Hey, that's right. If she'd been holding a bouquet of sagebrush, we wouldn't know for sure, would we?"

Meggie gave Paige a blank look, then picked up her can of pop and took a drink.

"We still don't know about her tin of treasures, though," Paige said, drinking some juice from a carton. "Let's see if she's gonna tell us where she hid it." Paige reached for the diary.

"I'm really glad she's feeling better, though," Meggie went on. "She isn't coughing like she was. And she and Johnny are doing stuff together now."

"Yeah. Johnny seems nice, doesn't he?"

Meggie nodded. "She's lucky to have a friend like that."

Paige turned and held Meggie's gaze.

"Well, sure—I'm lucky too," Meggie said to Paige. "Yeah. Sure. Almost as lucky as Anna."

"Almost?"

"Well, gee Paige," Meggie threw up her hands, "you never made me any dough balls!"

Paige burst out laughing.

"Shhhh!" Meggie whispered, trying to smother her own giggles. "We gotta be quiet, remember?"

"Yeah, we don't want the guy following us to know we're back. If it's the Badman or a ghost though..."

"Paige?"

"Yeah?"

"Be quiet and read."

Paige shrugged and began reading the diary.

August 22, 1880

Mama finally fetched Doctor Summers. They're fretting about my coughing and fever. It's much worse, and I so wanted to be better! I haven't been able to go outside, even in the sunshine and it's frightfully dull. I can't even tend my garden anymore. Mostly I miss Johnny, though. Mama isn't keen on him visiting and tiring me. The doctor says I'm not contagus though, so I don't worry when Johnny tiptoes to the window while Mama's resting. But she'd never hear us with that noisy Stamp Mill pounding out the ore night and day. The only time it's quiet around Bodie is when there's an accident in the mines and then I get scared for Papa. When he walks in that door all dirty and safe, I vow I'll never complain about the Standard Stamp Mill and Mine again! I've even learned how to sleep much better. After I say my prayers loud as can be (so God can hear) I just stuff my ears with cotton!

Meggie wiped a stray tear and turned to Paige. "I'll never complain about Dad's hammering and noisy jig saws and stuff again. Ever. He can stay out in the garage and make all the birdhouses he wants. Even past midnight."

"Yeah, I could loan you my ear plugs if you don't have any." Paige hesitated, then gazed hard into Meggie's face. "I wish I had a dad to stay home and make noise in our garage."

Meggie caught her breath. She wished she hadn't got started

on the subject of Dads. Meggie knew it was hard for Paige when everybody started talking about their dads since Paige's dad left her and her mom and ended up marrying somebody else. "Does your Mom make noise and keep you awake?" Meggie asked, wishing she could think of something better to say.

"No, it's me. I drive her bonkers with my loud music. But I'm not going to let that happen anymore, Meggie."

Meggie felt glad.

"I'm gonna give her some ear plugs for her birthday," Paige told her.

Meggie turned to Paige and they locked eyes, then broke out laughing.

"Let's read on," she said finally, wondering if her watery eyes were from the laughing, or Anna, or Paige not having a dad at home anymore.

Paige picked up the diary and started reading again:

I just love it when Johnny comes. He tells me tales of when he once had a papa and all the wild and marveless things they'd do. Johnny is brave and wise and strong just like his papa. I told him where I hid my tin of treasures and he said he could find a much better place where no one would find it. I'm so glad, too. Since I've been feeling so wretched, I must make absolute sure it's safe and that no one will find it. Except God, of course. God could help himself to the dough balls or share my treasures with anyone he chooses. But if God ever came to Bodie, I'm sure he'd have more important things to do. It's still a such a frightful bad

place to live. Scoundruls and bad men are everywhere. But
they won't find my treasures now!

Paige's eyes were glassy as she set the diary down. Meggie
wondered if Paige was thinking about Johnny's papa—the papa
he didn't have anymore. Did Johnny's papa just die or was he
killed in a mine? Or did he just up and leave Johnny and his
mama like Paige's dad?

"Uh—he sure loved his dad, didn't he?" Paige said finally.

"You mean, Johnny?"

"Yeah."

Meggie nodded, wishing she could do something to help
Paige with those feelings that kept coming up whenever anybody mentioned a dad.

"Do you think Johnny would still love his dad like that, even
if he'd done something bad or left him and his mama?" Paige's
eyes searched Meggie's.

Meggie tried to find the right words, but there weren't any. "I
don't know, Paige."

Paige didn't say anything after that and Meggie knew it was
probably because she just needed to think. Needed to try to get
rid of some of those bad feelings she'd been carrying around for
a long, long time.

"I sure wish she wasn't getting sick again," Paige said finally,
getting back to Anna.

Meggie agreed. "She's been sick for too long."

"It sorta makes me feel scared to keep reading," Paige went
on. "It needs to have a happy ending like in Nancy Drew or

53

Amelia Bedelia and I'm not sure that's gonna happen."

"I'm not either."

"Why don't they do something, Meggie? I mean, can't they call a specialist or get X-Rays and stuff like that?"

"Paige..."

"Okay, so maybe they can't call 911 since they didn't have phones and they probably didn't have X-Ray machines either. But they need to do something, Meggie. They need to do something besides just call Dr. Summers. If that doctor was doing what he was supposed to be doing, she wouldn't be getting worse. Why can't they get a stagecoach and rush her to the Medical Center in Virginia City or Ohio or something? I can't believe this, Meggie. The Badman From Bodie is nothing compared to the bad things that're happening to Anna. And nobody's doing anything!"

Suddenly Meggie's stomach lurched. Some planks and boards in the far corner started moving upward like a corpse coming out of a wooden grave. Meggie had almost forgotten about the shadow. She had been so absorbed in Anna's diary, she hadn't been watching. Or listening. Her flesh crawled and she gripped the diary tighter. *Is it him returning? Is the Badman From Bodie returning?*

"Yeeow!" Paige yelled, leaping up like she'd been shot.

Meggie couldn't move. She couldn't breathe.

The boards groaned and creaked as the figure emerged from beneath the house.

It was too late to run. Too late....

Chapter 7

A dirty, scrubby kid stood up and grinned. "Scared you, did I?"

Still in shock, Meggie stared at the boy who couldn't have been more than eleven or twelve-years-old. He was short and plump with a grin that was stuck like molasses to his freckled face.

"I almost had a heart attack!" Paige exploded. "What're you doing spying on us like that?"

"Curious," he replied, brushing some gunk off his bare arms. His t-shirt was so dirty, Meggie couldn't even read the words in front. "Been watching you, though," he told them.

"So it was you all this time!" Meggie burst out, her words exploding like a box of possums that had been penned up for a week. "You...YOU!"

"Well, you can just leave," Paige ordered. "Now!"

"Whoa, wait a minute, guys." He waved his arms.

"Excuse me?" Meggie interrupted, gripping the diary so tight her knuckles were white. "You heard my friend. Leave."

"Hey, I just wanted to see what you found."

"It's none of your business," Paige said with a snort.

"It is my business, because I happen to live in Bodie."

Meggie caught her breath. "You live here?"

"For now, yes. And in case you didn't know it, anything you find stays in Bodie so you better turn it in to one of the rangers at the Museum. Here, give it to me. I'll turn it in for you."

Meggie drew back and stood her ground. *The little nerd is trying to get the diary.*

"It's a diary, isn't it? You're looking for some treasure. I heard." He leaned over and brushed the dust out of the dirt-brown hair that was now turning red.

"We said go." Paige stepped closer, swinging her arms like she was ready for a wrestling match at school. "GO!"

"Okay, but if you wanna know anything, look me up. I know Bodie inside out. I know about some treasures and secrets that would make your sneakers shiver. I may even know where to find that treasure you're looking for."

Meggie and Paige fell silent and watched him walk away.

"Do you think he really might know?" Paige grabbed Meggie's arm.

"Well, he didn't know about the diary so how could he know about the treasure?" Meggie snorted. "He's probably just saying that so that he can get his hands on it himself."

"Yeah."

"And he can't live here, Paige. Nobody lives in Bodie."

"Except some of the rangers," Paige reminded her. "They live in a few of those old shacks that're fixed up. Remember when we walked by and looked in the window at the guy who was shaving and smiling at himself in the mirror? He was probably a ranger."

Meggie blushed, remembering. How could she forget? She had been so embarrassed, she thought she was going to flat out faint right there under the guy's window.

"The kid is a Dweeb, Meggie. One hundred per cent D-W-E-E-B."

"Yeah, it's like he crawled up outta a cave or mine or something."

Paige paused, then turned to Meggie again. "Do you think a Dweeb is the same thing as an Urchin?"

Meggie's chin fell. "Urchin?"

"Yeah."

"That's what Anna said they called her friend Johnny."

Paige stared long and hard at Meggie. "I know, except this kid is nothing like Johnny Merritt. Nothing at all."

"Right."

"This kid is the type that'd cream you with his dough balls," Paige went on. "And I'll bet you anything he hates carrots. He probably feeds 'em to his dog under the table when his parents aren't looking."

Meggie agreed. "But he still said he lives here and that he knows a lot of secrets."

"We don't need that nerdy kid to tell us what's what. Just because he knows Bodie's secrets and stuff like that doesn't mean a thing. A Dweeb is a Dweeb."

Meggie nodded lamely, the silence stretching between them.

"You don't really think Dweebs and Urchins are the same thing, do you?" Paige said finally, plopping down on what must once have been a step.

"I hope not. I'd feel sorta guilty if that was the case."

"Yeah, me too." Paige brushed some dirt off her cutoffs and drew a deep breath. "Anna would know. She could've told us."

Meggie got up and walked over, sitting down beside her best friend. "I think she already has, Paige."

"Yeah, yeah. Okay." Paige rolled her eyes heavenward, throwing up her arms. "Okay, okay—so maybe we can talk to him. But I'd never make him a jacket."

Meggie turned to her best friend. "Good thing, since you can't even hem up your jeans."

Paige snorted.

Meggie jumped up and brushed off the seat of her cutoffs. "Let's go, then!" she burst out. "Let's find the mysterious Dwee—er kid from Bodie and see if he can make our sneakers shiver!"

Chapter 8

They found him over near the fenced-off area surrounding the Standard Mine. It looked as though he was trying to crawl inside a gopher hole.

"Hey," Paige spoke first.

The kid brushed some dirt off his face and out of his hair and looked up. "Oh, it's you. Hi."

"I hope we didn't interrupt anything important," Meggie said, wishing she could think of something more intelligent to say. But it was too late.

"Naw," he said. "Just messing around as usual."

"Oh—yes, that's nice," Paige said, adding a few more stupid words to the lame conversation that was going nowhere.

"Uh, we figured we'd take you up on your offer," Meggie said finally, getting right to the point. "We'll show you what we found if you show us what you found."

"A deal." He stood up and held out his hand. "Name's Johnny. Johnny Downing."

"Downing?" Paige almost fell over backwards. "You're not related to Ranger Downing, are you?"

"Yup. She's my big sister. I'm staying in her cabin for most of the summer. Who're you?"

"I'm Paige Morefield and this is Megan Bryson," Paige said, yanking Meggie's arm. "Meggie, can you believe this? He's actually related to that nice ranger."

Meggie struggled for words, turning her thoughts away from Anna's diary and back to the dirt-covered kid with freckles, red hair and light brown eyes. "Oh yeah, hi," she said finally. It was hard to believe he was related to Ranger Downing. *He looks more like an oversized ground hog than he does a park ranger's brother.* She felt a sudden rush of shame at her thoughts.

"I sure feel a lot better knowing you're related to her," Paige said. "Don't you, Meggie?"

"Huh? Oh yeah," Meggie replied, knowing the secret would probably be safer with a ranger's little brother than it would be with some kid they didn't know.

Then suddenly it hit her. He'll tell. He'll tell his big sister and they'll have to turn in the diary before they get the chance to find out what happens to Anna. And her treasures, if they're still here.

"We found a diary in that old shack," Paige said, the words tumbling out like spilled milk.

"Paige," Meggie said, grabbing her arm and squeezing tight. "Wait..."

"It was written by this girl who lived in Bodie," Paige went on. "Her dad worked in the mines. Anyway, she hid her box of treasures and we're trying to find them. Probably dough balls and stuff like that. I've never seen dough balls in my life, have you?"

Meggie's heart fell and she released her grip. *It's too late...*

"What's her name?" Johnny asked, moving closer. His eyes were bright, the sweat on his dusty face gleaming.

"We can't tell unless you promise to keep it a secret," Meggie put in quickly. She had to do something. "Until we leave. Then we'll give it to your sister. We'll tell her then." There. She said it..

"Right," Paige agreed. "That's part of the deal. Take it or leave it."

Meggie drew a deep breath, waiting.

"It's a deal," he said. "Now, what's her name?"

"Wait a minute!" Meggie blurted, turning to the red-haired kid who was getting information faster than a speeding bullet. "Wait a minute. You were supposed to have some information for us, remember?"

Paige nodded in complete agreement.

"Look, do you want to find the treasure or what?" he asked them both. "I'll help you. I've found some neat stuff in Bodie. The park service really likes me. They let me hang out just about anywhere if I make discoveries without disturbing anything. They want you to leave every rock and rusty can where you found it. I've learned how to be real careful."

Meggie and Paige fell silent. Without his cooperation Meggie knew they might not find anything.

"Do you have her name? That's where I have to start," he told them.

Meggie nodded, forming her words carefully. "Anna Louise Lockmoor. She tells God goodbye in 1879 when she leaves Ohio and comes to Bodie."

Johnny Downing shook his head.

"Then you never heard of her?" Paige asked, swiping back the dark fringe of hair that was beginning to stick to the sweat on her forehead.

"No. I mean, everybody around here knows that there was some girl who wrote those words in her diary, but nobody knows anything about her on account of nobody's found the diary. Until now."

Meggie's hopes fell.

"We keep her diary hidden back at that old place where you saw us," Paige went on. "That's where we found it. She's giving us a lot of information."

"We think that's where she lived," Meggie added, wondering if Johnny Downing was going to be any sort of help at all. "Do you know whose place that was?"

"Nope." He shook his head again. "But, I want some details. What exactly did she hide?"

"A box," Meggie said. "A box with her special things in it."

"She calls it her tin of treasures," Paige added.

The red-haired kid thought for a moment, then spoke again. "First I guess we need to find out if she stayed and kept it hid, or if she left Bodie and took it with her. Make sense?"

They both nodded.

"The place where we stopped reading is where she's getting sicker and it doesn't look like she's getting any better," Paige told him. "We're almost afraid to keep reading just in case it doesn't have a happy ending."

"It might not," he said with a shrug. "Most of the little kids who were born in Bodie died before they grew up," he told them. "If some disease didn't wipe 'em out, the winters did. Sometimes the snow gets to be twenty-feet deep up here in the Sierra Nevadas, and the winds can blow up to a hundred miles an hour."

Meggie swallowed hard, thinking about Anna wrapped up in her quilt trying to keep warm. Trout Lake got pretty cold in the winter, but we never had winds like that. Or cracks in our walls, either. No, Meggie realized, life in Trout Lake didn't even come close to how hard it must have been up here in the Sierra Nevada mountains. *I sure wish I could've given Anna my electric blanket.*

"Okay," Johnny said, breaking into her thoughts, "let's get started. First we'd better find out if she died here in Bodie."

Died? His words jarred Meggie and she drew back. She wasn't sure if she wanted to know.

"We better start with the cemetery," he told them. "The Bodie cemetery west of town."

Chapter 9

No. Not the cemetery. I don't want Anna to be there. I want Anna to grow old and be a grandma forever.

Johnny went on, his words forcing Meggie to face what she knew she had to face. "If she's not in the cemetery, then she probably left Bodie with her things. Including her treasures. But if she's buried up there, then you'll know she stayed. If we find her tombstone in the cemetery, then there's a good chance her treasures might still be hid somewhere."

Cemetery. "No..." Meggie drew back, feeling that same uneasy feeling she got every time Aunt Abby's van passed the graveyard and drove into Bodie. "No, I don't like that place. I don't like cemeteries. I don't want to go there. Anna isn't there."

Johnny shrugged. "Have it your way."

"Besides, we have to go," she went on, glancing at her watch. "It's almost five. We have to meet my aunt at the parking lot." Her words were tight, her stomach knotted.

Meggie couldn't get out of there fast enough. She and Paige hurried away, skirting rocks and rusted metal and rotting boards. She passed the jail and the crumbling brick remains of the vault of the Bodie Bank and felt a chill. Death and rot lay everywhere.

Cemetery. Anna. No. She wanted to shut out Johnny's words— to bury those thoughts. Not a graveyard. No...

"Let's just read a little bit more, Meggie." Paige slowed down as they neared Anna's house. "Maybe it's gonna get better. Maybe Anna gets well and has a garden every spring and grows up and marries Johnny. We don't have to meet Aunt Abby this minute. Come on, Meggie. We have to know. I'm not gonna sleep very well if I don't know what happens."

Meggie hesitated. Maybe Paige was right. Maybe not knowing was going to be harder than knowing. She wasn't sure.

"I'll bet they had a whole bunch of kids who all loved carrots," Paige went on.

"Paige..."

"Well, let's find out."

Her best friend led the way over the remains of the old house and pulled out the diary. The late afternoon sun beat hot against them, even as they sat beneath the shade of the makeshift lean-to and began to read.

October 10, 1880

Dr. Summers comes nearly every day now. But so does Johnny. Miss Whitcomb is sending my schoolwork home with him, so I can do my lessons. Imagin. Johnny Merritt going to school every day! I think he's doing it on account of no one else wants to carry my books so far, though. Especially now that the weather is getting colder again. But

Johnny doesn't seem to mind. Besides, that way we get to visit more and do our recitations together. Why—he can recite "The Wreck of the Hesperus" almost better than I can! Miss Whitcomb thinks it's a pure miracle and even his ma can't believe how much he's changed. Sometimes he has to leave when I start coughing, though. He seems so sad then. How I wish I could take the sadness from his eyes and see the smiles again. Perhaps if I give him my locket with my picture inside, that might help some. He won't hanker to wear it of course, but if anything happens to me, he can always keep my picture and remember me. Yes, when he comes tomorrow, I'll tell him that if anything happens to me, he must fetch my locket from my tin of treasures and keep it for always and ever.

Meggie closed the diary, stray tears making little trails down her dusty cheeks. "Uh, guess we'd better go, huh?" she said finally, taking off her glasses and wiping them off with her t-shirt.

Paige nodded and turned away. If there were any tears, Meggie knew Paige wouldn't want her to see. Paige kept most of her feelings to herself, especially the sad ones.

After they had returned the diary to its hiding place, they walked back to where Aunt Abby was waiting. Meggie was glad her aunt was all hyped up over the artifacts she'd found at the mine. Listening to her aunt talk about her latest discoveries helped them both get their mind off Anna and the diary. But she knew it was going to be hard to sleep and get Anna out of her mind.

"I don't even care about The Badman From Bodie anymore," Paige said, crawling into her sleeping bag after the sun had gone down and the clouds covered the moon.

"Yeah. I don't either."

"And from now on I'm gonna eat my vegetables instead of feeding them to Fang under the table."

"Paige..." Meggie zipped up the tent and turned to her best friend.

"But I'm probably not gonna plant a garden, are you, Meggie?"

"I'm not sure."

"Last time I helped Grandma in the garden I got a slug in my hair and I didn't even know it until we were having lunch and it fell into my chicken noodle soup."

"That's gross, Paige."

"Now I hate chicken noodle soup."

"Yeah, can't say as I blame you."

"Every time I see one of those little noodles..."

"Paige."

"Okay, yeah. Well, night, Meggie."

"Night, Paige."

Bodie School

Chapter 10

Just as the van rounded the curve and headed into Bodie the next morning, Meggie accidentally glanced up at the cemetery on the left and saw Johnny Downing. She drew a quick breath and looked again, just to make sure. Yes. It was him. *That little nerd is already up there snooping around.* His red hair hit the sun like a neon sign.

"Now don't forget, girls," Aunt Abby cut into Meggie's furious thoughts, "we leave first thing tomorrow morning, so do everything you want to do. It's your last day at Bodie."

But all Meggie could think about was Johnny Downing snooping around up in the cemetery. "Paige!" she said the second Aunt Abby drove off. "It's him! He's up in that graveyard!"

Paige whirled around. "Huh? Who? The Badman From Bodie?"

"No, Paige. Johnny Downing! He's already groveling around up there," Meggie spit out the words like they were poisoned darts.

Paige shielded her eyes from the morning sun, gazing across the road and up toward the old graveyard on the hill. "He's cheating."

Meggie nodded, the heat rising up her neck.

"He's cheating, Meggie. That nerd is gonna find out all about her. He's gonna try and find her treasures before we do!"

"I know..."

"We have to go up there, Meggie!"

"No." Meggie drew back. "No, I don't—want to. There's gotta be rattlesnakes crawling all over those tombstones an—and besides, you know I have this thing about graveyards."

"Meggie, we have to!"

Meggie bit her lip and drew back again, shaking her head. "No. No, we don't."

"Okay, then I'll go up there myself!" Paige turned and tromped across the parking lot and back up the road toward the wooden gate at the foot of the hill.

Meggie watched her, watched her march straight up toward those tombstones. Why can't I do that? she said between clinched teeth. Why does Paige always have to be the brave one? Meggie hated the chicken-wimp side of her, but there didn't seem to be a thing she could do about it. She must have been born with it. Sort of like being born hating broccoli. *Wait a minute, Meggie Bryson. Wait a minute... Think about somebody else for a change, okay?*

All of a sudden Meggie saw Anna in her mind. Anna. *What happened to you, Anna? What happened?* She felt her back straighten, then threw back her shoulders and braced herself against the lamp post at the edge of the parking lot. *Okay, Anna. I'm gonna do this. If it wasn't for you, I'd let Paige go by herself. But I'm gonna do this for you. For you, Anna.*

The heat was already beating down on the dry desert

ground, yet Meggie knew her sweat wasn't coming from the sun. She drew a deep breath, then followed Paige up the path toward the graveyard, entering through a rickety revolving metal gate. Old tombstones stood like pale little ghosts, some with broken, crumbling wooden fences encircling them. Some headstones had fallen, battered by winds and time. Some were of marble and stone, some of wood. Meggie shivered and looked around, holding her head up, her chin firm. *You're not here, are you Anna. I know you're not here.*

Paige had already reached Johnny and they were deep in conversation by the time Meggie reached them.

"He says he can't find her tombstone anywhere," Paige said, turning to Meggie. "He's been here for an hour."

Meggie felt a sudden rush of relief.

"She still might be in an unmarked grave, though," he went on.

Meggie's hopes fell.

"Or maybe her headstone was made of wood and is rotted now. Another possibility is that it could've been stolen. A lot of 'em have been. But if she was buried in Bodie, she might be in the miners' section. Didn't you say her dad was a miner?"

Paige nodded, her hair whirling like a little dust devil in the morning breeze.

Or she could be buried right here where you're standing," Johnny said, gesturing in a circle. "This was called the Ward section and was where the ordinary, everyday people were buried."

Anna wasn't ordinary. No wonder she's not here.

"This section belonged to Mr. Ward, the undertaker. They named it after him," he went on. "Just north of here is where they buried the Chinese people. And over there are the Masons and their families." Johnny was pointing and talking like he knew this place inside out—like he was a half-pint ranger leading a tour. "On that side is where they buried the families belonging to the miners' union. And out there—outside the fence is Boot Hill."

"Boot Hill?" Meggie turned and gazed at the dry, desolate landscape beyond.

"Yeah. That was for the murderers and bad people."

"Was The Badman From Bodie buried out there?" Paige asked, gazing on the barren, rocky terrain.

"Who knows? But if he was, you probably couldn't find him. Nothing much but sagebrush out there, now. I guess nobody wanted to remember those people so they didn't put up any headstones that I know of."

"Did they bury Urchins out there?" Paige went on, her voice dropping, her eyes wide.

"Paige..."

"Urchins?" Johnny blinked against the sun's glare and tipped his head in question.

"Kids who wore rags and lived on the bad side of town."

"He wasn't one, Paige. Johnny Merritt wasn't an Urchin," Meggie cut in. "That's what some people called him, but Anna didn't. She knew the truth."

"I know, but I just wanted to be sure he wasn't out there, Meggie."

"Johnny Merritt?" It was Johnny speaking now.

"Oh yeah, he's her friend. Anna's friend," Paige told him.

Johnny fell silent, then spoke. "He—uh, he's got my name. Johnny..."

Paige cut in. "I know. But he's not at all like..."

Meggie silenced Paige with a sharp glance. "Uh, so what next?" she said to Johnny.

"Maybe we need to read more in that diary before we make the next move," he replied, his interest clearly mounting.

Meggie fingered her hair absently. One minute she wanted to get rid of Johnny Downing and the next, she didn't. He definitely wasn't a Dweeb, but on the other hand, Paige was right. He wasn't anything like Johnny Merritt, either.

"Okay," Paige said, turning on her heel. "So let's go."

Meggie didn't figure on hanging around to argue the point. She whirled around and started weaving around the headstones and broken-down gates and fences like she was in an obstacle course. Suddenly she stopped. A small white tombstone with a little hand-carved dove caught her eye. Meggie drew a deep breath and stared at the words.

EVA M. DAUGHTER OF J.Z. & A. LOCKWOOD.
DIED MAR. 12, 1892. AGED 11 YEARS. 5 MOS 2 DAYS.
ASLEEP IN JESUS, BLESSED SLEEP.

Her pulse pounded. For a minute she thought it was Anna...

"I wonder what happened to her?" Paige said, coming up from behind. She paused for a moment and shook her head as she read the words etched in stone. "Gee, Meggie, that girl was practically the same age as Anna..."

Meggie bit her lip and turned away. *I don't want to think*

about it. No...

Johnny had passed them and was heading down the hill toward the road that led into Bodie.

"Where's he going?" Meggie said to Paige finally.

"To Anna's house, I guess. To read more and find out what happened."

Meggie drew back.

"It's time, Meggie. We have to leave Bodie tomorrow and if we don't find out what happened before we go, we won't ever know."

Meggie's throat tightened as she stared across the road toward the ghost town where Anna once lived. Bodie—the town where Anna Louise Lockmoor planted her daisies and hauled the wood—where the winds howled like terrible wolves outside her door when the winter snows fell...

The barren landscape blurred before her eyes. The ghost town lay like wooden bones across the brown desert floor, waiting to come back to life.

A coyote howled somewhere in the distance.

Yes, Anna. It's time.

Bodie Cemetery

Chapter 11

November 3, 1880.

It's getting terrible cold again, but Johnny still comes every day after school. I feel so tired now but I shant ever fall asleep when he comes. He makes me so happy and promises my treasures will be safe in the special hiding place near the creek. He says he's going to go there as often as he can before the snows come to make sure the tin is snug and dry. He told me that next to coming here to be with me, he likes to spend time there best. Johnny says that when he sits on that rock and watches the water tumbling over the stones, he finds quiet for his heart. How I wish I had the strength to go there, too. But even here underneath my scratchy quilt, I'm starting to find that same quiet for my heart too. Oh, rough little creek, stay close to Johnny always! Show him you are really dancing and singing along your rocky path. Saying Hello. Saying Goodbye...

And then it ended.

"Wait a minute!" Paige choked, thumbing through the blank

pages. "Where's the rest?"

Meggie couldn't answer. She felt the words backing up in her throat. *She was saying goodbye. Anna was saying goodbye...*

"It was...didn't—didn't you see?" Paige sputtered on, brushing a stray tear off her cheek.

"Gone. Ripped out," Johnny said, taking the words right out of her mouth. "A page is missing. Go—gone." His words were quivering like his baggy t-shirt in the fresh morning wind.

Paige's eyes were huge and watery, her hands trembling. "How come? That's not fair. Now we won't know."

"Maybe we will," Johnny held his voice steady.

Meggie took the diary from Paige and turned, trying to keep her thoughts and her words even. "H-How, Johnny?" she said carefully, holding back the feelings that were ready to spill out all over her cheeks. They had to know.

"I'm not sure, except I think I know where he hid that box of treasures," Johnny told them.

"You do?" Paige moved closer.

Meggie listened closely, trying to quiet the thumping of her heart long enough to hear his words.

"Rough Creek. It's a few miles up the road from here, but I know a short cut. After the town wells dried up, that was where Bodie got a lot of its water."

"Rough Creek?" Paige gripped the diary and opened to the last entry once again. "Whoa, okay—here it is... *my treasures will be safe in the special hiding place near the creek.* She moved her finger down the page and went on, *Rough little creek, you are really singing and dancing...*Oh wow! You think that's it, Johnny?"

"Can you take us there?" Meggie put in, her sinking thoughts struggling upward now. There was hope. *Even if we don't know what happens to her, at least maybe we'll find her treasures—at least we'll have something that belonged to her. Something to touch. Something to remember.*

"Yeah, I'll take you there." he said with a nod. "We can make it in a little over an hour if we move."

Meggie slipped the diary back into the copper tin and slid it back down into its hiding place, then followed Johnny and Paige. Dust flew as they cut through Bodie, then crossed the road. Little dust devils spun like tiny tornados across their path, luring them on.

"You won't have to worry too much about rattlesnakes up here," he told them as they began the short-cut up the mountain. "Too much elevation. Probably only a few crawling around."

Rattlesnakes. Meggie choked, trying to keep up with Paige who was climbing and leaping over sagebrush like they were low hurdles on the school track.

"Bodie's really cool," he went on, brushing his red hair from his eyes. "I come here almost every summer."

"Yeah?" Paige said breathlessly. "Then do you know anything about The Badman From Bodie?"

The Badman From Bodie? Meggie's thoughts shifted as she listened to Johnny.

"Only that nobody knows who he was so they just figure he was probably a whole bunch of bad guys put together," Johnny said. "But I think he might've been Washoe Pete or Dog Face George."

Meggie drew a deep breath and brushed some dust off her face. "Dog Face George? Yeah, I remember. We walked past his house the first day we came to Bodie."

"Who was he?" Paige asked, catching up to Johnny.

"An old guy who lived on the edge of town. His place is still there."

"Was he bad?" Paige went on, her short dark hair whirling in the soft, dusty wind. She was at Johnny's side, glued to his words.

"I'm not sure," Johnny said. "But I think he was."

"He—he doesn't still live there, does he?" Paige asked, glancing down over her shoulder.

"Naw, he's probably six feet under up there in Boot Hill."

"You sure? I mean, you said there aren't any headstones, so how would anybody know for absolute positive sure?"

Johnny shrugged. "He'd have to be pretty old."

"Well, I know *real* old antique-type people who go dancing and climb mountains and all kinds of stuff like that," Paige told him. "This old guy sitting on the porch at the Trout Lake Grange almost creamed me with his cane when I told him to take it easy."

Meggie giggled.

"No kidding, Meggie," Paige frowned, "He was serious. It scared me to death."

Johnny shook his head and hiked on, leading the way through a draw, then on up toward the ridge. "Who knows, maybe Dog Face George does still hang out around these parts..."

Meggie plodded on, feeling her sweat against her shirt, listening as Johnny told them his version of the Dog Face George legend. They hiked on and on up the mountain, and when they finally reached the crest, a rush of cooler air gave some relief from the heat. Thoughts of Dog Face George faded as Meggie gazed down at the small creek tumbling through the valley.

"Whoa!" Paige exclaimed, pointing to the path of water below. "Is that it? Is that Rough Creek?"

Johnny nodded, leading the way downward.

As they neared the bottom of the ravine, Meggie scanned the dry, grassy terrain that followed the creek, looking for the rock where Johnny Merritt might have sat—the rock where he might have hidden Anna's treasures. Tall, white-barked aspen lined the banks, waving a welcome with their yellow, shimmering leaves, and on the distant ridge beyond, a few cows grazed on the prairie grass.

"From what she said in the diary, he probably hid her treasures in the same rock where he used to sit," Johnny told them.

Meggie agreed. Where else could he have stashed it? Except for the yellow-leafed aspens and a few cows, the place was as bare as an old tin wash tub. *I just hope he didn't bury it, though, because if he did, we probably won't find it.*

They agreed to search in opposite directions, meeting back at the starting point in half an hour.

Meggie and Paige hiked up the craggy, winding creek bed, searching for the rock where Johnny Merritt sat and found his peace. The noise of the rushing water covered up the churning of her stomach as they hiked on and on. Finally, Meggie slowed down and glanced at her watch. It was almost noon and she was starved. Yanking a sandwich from her pack, she followed Paige around a bend.

"Whoa, look at that!" Paige cried. She had taken the lead and was pointing to a large rock on the far side of the creek. "You think that's it, Meggie? Look! It's big enough to sit on!"

Meggie glanced up and drew a deep breath, stuffing her sandwich back down into her backpack. Yes! Yes! The shale rock jutted up like a small, flat-topped mountain, causing her head to spin with hope. *Is that it, Johnny? Is that the rock you sat on?*

Paige didn't wait for Meggie to answer. Leaping over rocks, she crossed the creek. Water splashed and danced around Meggie's feet as she followed Paige across Rough Creek. Her throat felt dry, but it wasn't because she was hungry and thirsty anymore.

In seconds they were circling the huge rock with its flat, sloping top, checking every crevice where Johnny might have hidden the box.

Suddenly, Meggie spotted a crack half way up—a large crack where a wide slice of rock appeared to have been wedged in tight. She gasped, then started to pull, trying to loosen the stone. "Pa—Paige!" she cried. "Paige...I think I found it!"

Chapter 12

Rocks flew as Paige skidded to a halt, breathing down Meggie's neck.

"I think it's in there! Oh, Paige, I'm almost sure Anna's treasures are in there!" Meggie was almost choking on her excitement, trying to talk, trying to pull out the wedge of rock and get a closer look.

But the rock wouldn't budge.

"Wait..." Meggie drew back and grabbed her flashlight out of her pack. Struggling to hold her hand steady, she shone the light into the narrow crack. "Look, Paige! Look! I think I see something!" Her words tumbled out like the water rushing along the creek bed beside them.

Paige crouched down beside Meggie and strained to get a closer look. "Yes...yes!" Paige exploded.

"Oh, Paige! I can't believe it. I just can't..."

"We have to get the stupid rock out first!" Paige sputtered, grabbing and struggling with all her might.

"I know. I know!" Meggie was almost dancing now. "Didn't Johnny do a fantastic job of hiding her treasures? They're still here, Paige. After more than a hundred years, Anna's treasures are still here!"

Paige nodded, sweat running down her arms as she pulled and yanked at the stubborn rock. "But it's not coming, Meggie. This freaky rock is stuck!"

Meggie crouched back down, struggling once again to move the unyielding wedge of stone Johnny Merritt had forced into the cool, dark hiding place. But time and wind and sand had sealed up Johnny's hiding place until now. It was almost as tight as a tomb.

By this time, Paige had found a sharp stone and began working it into the crack. But it still didn't move. The rock seal refused to budge.

"Hey, we're supposed to meet Johnny," Meggie said, glancing at her watch. "We're late!"

Paige looked up and wiped the sweat from her dusty face and wide brown eyes. "Maybe he's got a knife or something..."

"Let's go!" Meggie cried, whirling around and leading the way back to where they had agreed to meet.

"What's up?" Johnny asked, getting up from the rock where he had been waiting. As usual, he looked like he had just finished rolling in the dirt. "Did you find something?"

"Yeah," Meggie nodded, yanking her pack off her shoulders and grabbing a soda. "I think we did!"

Johnny's chin fell.

Meggie opened her pop and gulped down the liquid. She felt almost dizzy with thirst. And excitement.

"We found this humungous rock," Paige told him, breathing

hard. "And a big crack with a rock stuck in it. Like a hiding place sealed shut."

"Whoa!" Johnny burst out, heading downstream. "Show me!"

Paige reached for a soda and caught up with Meggie and Johnny, weaving around the aspen and jumping over small rocks and scrub along the bank. "Want one?" she asked Johnny who had clearly caught the excitement of their new discovery.

He nodded, taking the soda like a hand-off in a relay.

In a few minutes they had reached the rock.

"Hey, cool!" Johnny said, slowing down and circling it. His light brown eyes were flashing, scanning the thing like a hawk scouting its prey.

Meggie motioned him over to the crevice with the rock-seal.

Sweat poured down Johnny's dusty face as he reached into his rear pocket and pulled out his pocket knife. He rammed his knife into the crevice, prying and pulling, but the wedge still wouldn't move.

"It's in there," Meggie told him. "We're almost positive Anna's tin of treasures is behind that piece of rock!"

Johnny sweated and worked in vain.

"Let's break for a sec," Paige said, finally, plopping down on the creek bank and pulling out some chips and cookies. "I'm starved."

Meggie agreed, sitting down beside her. "But we have to hurry. There isn't much time left if we're leaving Bodie this afternoon! Ohhh, I just wish we could stay one more day!" She pulled out some sandwiches and handed one to Paige and another to Johnny. Her hand trembled.

"I brought extra," she said to Johnny.

"Thanks."

Meggie had actually brought the extra food along for the rabbits, but Johnny probably deserved it after all he was doing to help.

"You're not a Dweeb," Paige said, biting down into her half-smashed sandwich.

Meggie stiffened.

"Huh?" Johnny looked up, his freckles blending with the dirt covering his face.

"You sorta look like one at times, but you're not," Paige went on, chewing her peanut butter sandwich like she was in a sandwich-eating contest at the Fair.

"A what?" Johnny asked again, the hot sun beating down on his dusty red hair.

"Uh—a Beeb, Johnny. We—we didn't bring a Beeb," Meggie put in, her cheeks flushing crimson.

"What's a Beeb?" He seemed confused now.

"It uh—might've worked better than a knife, though, don't you think, Paige?" Meggie went on, her words bumbling and banging around like the creek beside them. "But we don't have a Beeb, and your jack knife doesn't work, so we have to think of something else."

"A Beeb?" Now Paige seemed confused. "I said a Dw..."

"Yeah, Paige. A BEEB."

"Oh yeah, a Beeb," Paige said, catching Meggie's sharp glance. "A Beeb definitely won't work."

Johnny finished his sandwich, still looking confused. "Let's see if we can find something to pry that rock open," he said, getting up. "I think this is private land so maybe we can find a barn or shed and borrow some tools. Or maybe some old pipe that used to carry water from this creek down to Bodie. Except I think maybe the pipe they used then was made out of wood."

"We'll find something," Paige said, grabbing some chocolate chip cookies before she got up.

"Keep cool, though," Meggie added. "If this is private land, we don't want anybody to get suspicious. We need to find this ourselves and if..."

But before she had finished her sentence, she heard a weird, rustling noise just behind them.

Paige and Johnny had heard it, too. Meggie reeled around and froze. A sudden burst of dust exploded, then disappeared behind a ridge.

Someone is following us!

Chapter 13

Paige turned as white as a ghost. "Whaa?"

Johnny motioned her quiet.

Meggie's pulse pounded. She groped for Paige's arm, squeezing it until her fingers felt numb.

"You don't think it's The Badman From Bodie or Dog—Dog Face George, do you?" Paige almost choked. Her eyes were as round as the chocolate chip cookies she'd just dropped on the ground. "Or that other guy..."

"Paige, are you serious?" Meggie released her grip.

"Well, it could be, Meggie. In case you forgot, Bodie is a ghost town. Weird things can happen in or around ghost towns..."

"Shhh!" Johnny ordered.

Meggie pushed Paige's words from her mind. "Maybe it was just a coyote," she said to Johnny, hoping Paige was one-hundred percent wrong.

"I don't think so," he said carefully, trying to hold his words steady. "Coyotes are too small to make that much noise—that much dust." He was shading his eyes against the sun, gazing up the creek valley toward the ridge. "Maybe it was just a cow."

Meggie gulped and noticed his face had turned from shades

of brown to pale green. No. She knew Johnny wasn't sure about the cow either.

"So what now?" Paige asked, her face still pale, her eyes huge.

"Well, it's gone now. Whatever it was, it's gone."

Meggie bit her lip and watched Johnny back away and motion for them to follow him up the other side of the ridge.

"Come on," he said, "let's try to find a tool or something!"

Meggie wiped the sweat from her face and shook her head. "Wait a minute. We'd better not leave this rock, Johnny. What if somebody saw us trying to get that thing out? They might come back as soon as we're out of sight. They might find Anna's treasures first."

"You've got a point. Yeah, okay, then you stay here and I'll go look," he told them. "Just sit on that rock like you're daydreaming or whatever. It—it was probably just a cow, anyhow."

I hope he's right.

"I'll find something," he went on, backing up. "I can uncover or dig up just about anything."

Meggie believed him. He almost always looked like he'd just crawled out of a mine shaft or a gopher hole.

Meggie began scouting around the brush, while Paige waited near the rock. Both were silent, watching for any movement—listening for any sounds. But there was nothing. No one.

Meggie moved up the bank, looking for some metal—an old pipe—anything. *We have to hurry. There's not much time left.* Overhead, clouds worked their way across the sky. The hot shiver of wind made her sweat cold as the barren hills trembled in the heat. Except for the gurgling, rushing creek and a few lonely coyotes in the distance, it was quiet. Eerie.

Suddenly Meggie saw a flash of metal. Quickly she made her way toward the object. Her heart leaped. A piece of an old pipe with a ragged, knife-like point lay nearly hidden in the scrub. "Awesome!" she burst out, grabbing the iron tool and racing back to the rock.

Paige rushed toward her. "What'd you find?"

Meggie waved the rusty thing like a flag, ramming it into the crack until her knuckles whitened.

"What is it?"

"An old pipe, I think," she said, breathing hard as she worked the sharp edge into the narrow slit. "Whoa...yeah! I think it's gonna work, Paige!"

Breathing down her neck, Paige cried out. "Oh, Meggie! Yes—Yes!"

Meggie forced and strained with all her might until the rock started to move. Oh please—PLEASE! The sweat of her excitement felt cold against the hot wind encircling them. "Yes! Yes...it's moving, Paige!"

Paige threw her hand over her mouth, her eyes huge.

Meggie bit her lip, straining—pushing. But it still wouldn't come. Not quite...

"Here, let me try," Paige said, taking the tool from Meggie's sweaty hands. She groaned and struggled, but the stubborn wedge of rock wasn't giving up without a fight.

Suddenly, a thought hit Meggie's mind. Her heart fell. Maybe we're not supposed to take her treasures. Meggie braced herself against the rock, remembering Anna's words. *I must make sure it's safe and that no one will find it. Except God. God could help himself to the dough balls or share my treasures with anyone he chooses.*

"Oh, Paige," she said, almost choking on the words, "d—do you th—think maybe we're not..."

But just before Meggie could finish, Paige exploded in one final burst of strength and the huge rock-wedge came flying out.

"Yahooo!" she exploded, leaping aside as it crashed on to the ground. "We did it! We did it, Meggie Bryson!"

Meggie lowered herself slowly, bracing herself against the rock. She gazed into the dark hole and saw it. It was there. *I can't believe this. I can't...* There were no words right then. Nothing except the wild pounding of her heart, the wild thumping inside her shirt that was almost deafening. Oh, Johnny! Anna! I can't believe this...

Anna's tin of treasures was still here—still in this rock where Johnny Merritt had hidden it over a hundred years before.

Suddenly Paige muffled a scream.

Meggie whirled around. "Whaaa..."

"Some—Somebody's coming!" Paige's uneven words struck like a menacing vulture circling. She was pointing. Another cloud of dust had stirred on ridge to their right. Again.

Oh no... Meggie backed up against the huge rock, unmoving. She caught Paige's wide, flashing eyes. Fear gripped them both—held them hard against the rock.

It can't be Johnny. No. It's too soon for him to be coming back. Besides, what would he be doing over there on the opposite side of the ridge? No. That wasn't Johnny Downing. It couldn't be....

A shot rang out.

Chapter 14

Paige and Meggie froze.

Fear circled Meggie's throat like a bull snake. She couldn't move. She couldn't breathe.

"Do—Dog—Faaaa..."

"Shhh!" Meggie choked.

Paige's eyes were huge and Meggie knew they were both thinking the same thing. But it can't be Dog Face George—no, it can't! Her mind raced. Or that other guy Johnny was talking about. NO! They're gone now. The Badmen From Bodie aren't here anymore. Sweat crawled down Meggie's neck and arms and face.

Suddenly two more shots exploded over the rise.

Meggie reached for Paige's arm and they clung to each other, trembling. Sweating. Glued like magnets to the cold, hard rock.

"Th—this is it." Paige's raw whisper trembled, blending with the sounds of creek beside them.

Suddenly Meggie heard footsteps hitting the rocky creek bed, coming closer and closer.

Oh no...NO... Meggie felt Paige's hand squeezing hers until it was numb. Is this what happened to him, too? Is this what happened to Johnny Merritt?

"Get down!" Johnny Downing cried out, racing across the creek toward them.

Johnny!

Pale, trembling, Johnny circled the rock and skidded to a halt, dirt and rocks flying. "I said get down!"

Meggie and Paige fell like boulders to the ground.

"We have to get outta here!" he cried, casting a frantic glance behind them. "Now!"

"Wait!" Meggie cried, jumping up. "The box! Anna's treasures!"

"No! We don't have time!" he blurted. "Somebody's shooting at us!"

Rocks flying, Paige spun around and retrieved the tin, holding it tight against her pounding heart.

Meggie gasped and stared unbelieving at the box that had belonged to Anna Louise Lockmoor. "Oh Paige! Paige!"

Johnny grabbed Meggie's shirt and yanked her out of her trance. "Paige! Meggie! Let's go!" he cried out, his face white with fear. "Now!"

Paige held Anna' treasures close and followed Johnny. Dark hair flying, she crossed Rough Creek, her small legs and feet a blur.

"Oh, Paige, be careful!" Meggie choked. "Be careful of Anna's things!" Meggie felt her long legs and feet slipping and sliding, water seething and churning in every direction. But Meggie knew that if anyone could hang on and run without falling, it would be Paige. Paige Morefield was fast and sure. Paige could run like the wind.

Johnny kept glancing over his shoulder, prodding them on. "Hurry!" he said as they retraced their steps back over the ridge above Bodie. "Hurry!"

Coyotes howled somewhere in the hills beyond, eerie little yip-yip-yips filling the air. The sun beat hot as they raced down the mountain at breakneck speed, rocks and brush flying. Meggie had never run so fast in all her life. She had never been so scared.

Finally, after what seemed like hours, they dropped down into a draw just long enough to catch their breath. The dry river bed wound like a snake just above Bodie and shielded them from anyone who might be on their trail. "We're alive!" Meggie cried, glancing over her shoulder. But for how long?

Paige still clung to the tin. Panting. Choking.

"He—he's not sh—shooting now..." Johnny stammered, peering over the rise behind them. "I—I don't see...him. We're close to Bodie now. This gully follows th—the road. I th—think we're safe."

But Meggie knew they wouldn't be safe, not until they were back in Bodie. Her chest heaved in and out as she tried to catch her breath—tried to think straight.

"Was—was it...Dog—Dogface...or the Ba—Ba...?" It was Paige now.

Johnny wiped the dust and sweat from his troubled brow with a trembling hand. "I—I don't know."

"But it could be, right?" Meggie said, staring hard into his face. "That shotgun…"

"No," he choked. "It wasn't a shotgun. It—it was a pistol. And he…"

"Who?" Paige grabbed him. "Who, Johnny?"

"Washoe Pete."

"Wh—Who's *that*?" Meggie exploded.

"He—Washoe Pete was—was probably the Badman. Th—The Badman From Bodie!" Johnny exploded. His face and neck were as red as his hair.

"But, how do you know that wa—was him shooting?" Meggie cried, trying to keep her voice down, trying to keep her thoughts clear.

"The shots…the gun," he said, still glancing up over the edge of the ditch. "It sounded like a British Bull-Dog…"

"No! No, Johnny! Don't throw in a dog!" Paige exploded. "The Badman and Wash hole Pete, they're enough! We don't need a dog too!"

"The British Bull-Dog is a pistol. His favorite."

"Who's favorite?" Meggie gasped.

"Washoe Pete. He kept it in his right coat pocket. The pocket was lined with velvet buckskin so the hammer wouldn't catch." Johnny's breath came fast, his words still hot with fear.

"Is he still alive?" Paige grabbed him again, her eyes as wide as the huge sun falling down the sky.

"Uh, well some people say he still hangs out over the eastern Sierras."

"Oh no…" Meggie gasped, grabbing the tin from Paige and jumping up. She held Anna's tin of treasures close to her thudding heart. "We have to get outta here! NOW!"

They took off running once more and didn't slow down until they reached the town of Bodie sprawled like a heap of bones across the valley of pale green sage and rock.

"Oh, my gosh, we made it!" Meggie cried. "We made it!" They were leaning against the stone stage depot across the road from the parking lot. Safe! Alive.

"Open it!" Paige exploded, reaching for Anna's tin.

Meggie hesitated, glancing around, then motioned Paige and Johnny behind the building where they would be out of sight.

She drew a careful breath and crouched down, staring at the tiny hand-painted flowers sprinkled like a wild garden on the tin box. *Oh Anna. I can't believe it. I just can't believe it...* The flowers were pale now, faded by time. Her heart still pounded, but now Meggie knew it wasn't fear.

This was the moment she and Paige had been waiting for— the moment that almost never came.

Chapter 15

Meggie's hands trembled as she began to open the lid. *This is it, Anna. Your treasures.* She could hardly believe it was really happening.

"Here, let me, too," Paige said, kneeling beside her. Her words trembled, her eyes glistened.

Together, they worked it open while Johnny Downing stared open-mouthed above them.

"Whoa..." Paige almost fell over backwards as the lid popped open. "Will you look at this?"

Meggie gasped, staring in awe at the tiny handmade marbles still bright with glaze and color. Dough balls. Johnny and his ma had painted those. Tears stung her lids as she fingered the marbles and the little red and white checkered tea set with tiny flowers painted on the cups and saucers. *Oh Anna, did you play with these?* Carefully she fingered a tin cup and saucer, then a small, brightly-painted yellow stove made of iron. Or was it copper? Beneath the little stove lay a packet of seeds. Daisies. *But weren't you going to plant those in the spring?* Meggie's throat tightened and her eyes welled up.

A tiny porcelain doll dressed in a calico dress lay twisted among the treasures—a broken leg and arm beside her. Meggie watched as Paige straightened the ruffle so that it covered the leg that wasn't there. *I'm sorry, Anna. I hope we didn't do this.* The little doll blurred before Meggie's eyes and she turned away. Then Meggie opened a small, well-worn Bible inscribed: "To Anna, With Love from Mama and Papa." She swallowed her tears and closed it. *Oh Anna. You're here. You're here with us right now, aren't you?*

"Meggie..." Paige's words trembled like the wind. "It's not here, Meggie."

Eyes brimming, Meggie turned to Paige.

"The last page in her diary. It's not here."

Meggie shook her head, wiping a stray tear. No. No, it wasn't. If only they could have known her last words. If only they could have known what happened.

Johnny turned away. Meggie knew he couldn't keep the feelings back either. None of them could. None of them had any words. There was so much inside Meggie right then and there wasn't any way to get it out. But Anna was there with them all. The small, precious objects blurred before Meggie's eyes as the words came back: *I must make sure it's safe and that no one will find it. Except God, of course. God could help himself to the dough balls or share my treasures with anyone he chooses.*

God can share my treasures with anyone he chooses...

"This—this doesn't—belong to us, Paige," Meggie said, taking off her sunglasses and wiping her wet eyes. Her blonde hair circled in the soft wind, catching the late afternoon sun.

Paige looked hard into her face.

"You mean, put it back in that rock?" Johnny asked, his eyes searching Meggie's.

"No," she said carefully, knowing what they had to do. "No, I mean we share her treasures."

Paige picked up the tin and held it close. She knew.

And so did Johnny. He understood. They all understood.

"We can ask my sister if they'll put her treasures in the Museum—so nobody will ever forget her," he said quietly.

"Next to her picture," Paige added, blowing her nose on a paper napkin she had just pulled out of her back pack.

"Her picture?" Johnny turned to Paige.

Paige nodded. "In the Museum there's a picture of a girl holding some daisies. A ranger told us she was just an unknown girl from Bodie, but we know who she is. We're almost positive it's Anna."

It's time... Meggie said through the silent tears still running deep. *It's time to get Anna's things out of that dark place...*

Johnny took the tin from Paige's hands and opened the lid, gently moving his finger over each object.

Meggie turned to him. They hadn't meant to leave him out. In a way, Johnny Downing was an important part of all that was happening. "I hope you get a chance to read her diary," she said to him. "It sort of explains all this. I mean, even the little seeds and stuff. Anna has so much to say."

"I will," he said, looking up at Meggie. "I almost feel like I know her. Like she's...well, part of my life, too."

Meggie nodded, then drew a deep breath and glanced down

at her watch. "Oops, we'd better hurry! We've gotta turn all this in and meet Aunt Abby back here at the parking lot by five." Then she reached for the tin. "If it's okay, Johnny, Paige and I just need to take turns holding it as long as we can. We have to leave in the morning and we're not going to get to go to the Museum and look at it every day, like you."

"Sure," Johnny said, handing the tin to Meggie. He turned and started across the dirt road and through the parking lot toward the park office. "The rangers will take care of Anna and her things. My sister'll see to that. I know she will."

Meggie felt the lump again, but it was okay now. At least they were leaving Anna's treasures with Johnny and his sister in charge. *They'll take care of her things.*

"We have to turn in the diary, too, don't we," Paige said, turning to Meggie. It was a statement, not a question. They had already agreed they would turn it in before they left Bodie.

Meggie nodded reluctantly, wishing they didn't have to— wishing they could keep her diary and her treasures forever.

She sighed as she walked toward the park office, then noticed that Johnny had slowed down and was glancing nervously over his shoulder. Meggie's heart skipped a beat. In all the excitement, she and Paige had almost forgotten they were being followed. Shot at.

Meggie stopped and turned to Johnny. "You don't really think that was the ghost of Washoe Pete back there, do you?" she asked.

"I don't know."

Meggie felt confused. But they were safe now, weren't they?

Weren't they? Her skin prickled and she gripped the tin of treasures tighter in her hand.

Johnny caught up to her and shook his head, still confused.

"Who was it, then, Johnny?" she asked as they walked past the old church toward the Park Office.

"Maybe we'll never know."

Paige reached for the tin in Meggie's hand and ran her fingers across the tiny little wild flowers painted on top.

Meggie's thoughts shifted and her heart welled up. Those little flowers were so small and beautiful—still blooming just like Anna. Tears stung her lids. Soon they would have to say goodbye to her forever, wouldn't they? *I'm going to miss you, Anna. I'm really going to miss you.*

Meggie walked on past the Miller House, trying to keep the flood of tears from falling all over her face. But it wasn't easy. It wasn't easy to say goodbye.

When they reached the park office, Paige handed her the tin and together they held it one last time.

Johnny turned away and faced the pale, distant hills.

Finally, Paige handed him Anna's treasures.

Meggie's heart fell.

"Uh, I'll get my sister and—and we'll meet you over at Anna's house in a few minutes," he said to them both.

Meggie knew he meant they'd come for the diary. Yes. It was almost time to say goodbye forever to Anna Louise Lockmoor, wasn't it? She turned and began to walk away.

"Wait a minute," Johnny said. "What's a Beeb?"

Meggie caught her breath. *Oh no...*

"I think it might be what Barbie uses to fix her car," Paige said, holding his gaze. "Except I'm not positive since I don't play with Barbies anymore."

"Barbie?"

"You know, Barbie and Ken."

Johnny seemed confused again.

"We'll meet you at Anna's house," Meggie put in, grabbing Paige's arm.

As soon as Johnny was out of sight, Meggie turned to Paige. "Paige," she said, "don't ever..."

"I won't," Paige interrupted. "But if I do, I'll say Beeb instead of Dweeb."

"No, Paige."

"Okay, okay..." Paige threw up her hands and walked off.

Meggie dropped the subject and followed her best friend toward Anna's house.

"I sure wish we knew who was following us, though," Paige said finally, cutting past the town well, now covered with boards. "But if it had been that Wash hole Pete, we'd be zip, don't you think, Meggie?"

"WashHOE Pete..."

Paige rolled her eyes and walked on. "Three sixth-grade skeletons lying in the dust, waiting for the snow to bury them alive. Hey, isn't that what happened to the guy they named this town after? Water—Waterman Bodey. Yeah, that's it. Didn't his gold hunting partner find him after the snow melted the following Spring? That book we've got says the coyotes scattered his bones all over the hills. Thank goodness he wasn't twelve. It's bad enough they spelled his name wrong."

Meggie scarcely heard. They had almost reached Anna's house and thoughts of her returned like a gentle Bodie wind. Meggie stepped over the boards and junk lying around the back yard, then eased herself up on to the uneven floor of the house. Making her way across the planks to the hiding place, she retrieved the diary. The old copper tin crunched as she opened it and stared blurry-eyed at the leather-bound book inside.

Paige came up from behind and reached for the diary, gently thumbing through the yellowed pages. "I just don't see why somebody had to tear out the last page, though," she said to Meggie. "Now we're never gonna know what really happened."

Meggie stood in the shadows of the old house that had hidden Anna's diary all these years, knowing Paige was right. She drew a deep breath and gazed on the blurred horizon, watching the afternoon sun slide down the sky. The old dwellings were casting shadows, getting ready for another lonely night in the eastern Sierras.

"I guess we won't ever know if she was okay, will we Meggie?"

Meggie struggled with the tears still threatening to come, then turned to Paige. "I'm not sure, except—except remember what she said about the creek, Paige? About the creek dancing and singing?"

Paige paused and gazed into Meggie's face.

"Remember, Paige? *Rough little creek...show him you are really dancing and singing on your rocky path...*"

"Do you think she meant she was okay, Meggie? Like even though things were really hard, she was actually, well—almost...

happy?"

Meggie swallowed her tears and tried to smile. "I think so. I really think that's what she meant."

"That sure makes me feel a lot better," Paige said, her eyes glistening. "I guess we needed to find that diary when we did. I don't think it would've lasted too much longer anyway. I mean, this place is falling apart and the cold winds and storms and stuff would've wiped everything out, don't you think? Diary and all."

"Maybe not. Maybe nothing could ever destroy Anna."

"Oh, Meggie..."

Meggie reached for the diary and ran her fingers over the worn black leather with its tarnished brass latticed corners. Her throat tightened as she gazed around at the falling structure that might have been her house—at the yard now littered with trash and boards. Was this where Anna hauled water and fixed potatoes for dinner? Was this where she and Johnny played with the dough balls...where she planted her garden?

Tears stung her lids as she stared at the precious book in her hands. If this was Anna's house, did she hide this under a loose floorboard in her bedroom? Or maybe the kitchen? Maybe she hid this under the woodbox by the stove where she always helped her mom. Meggie could almost see Anna hauling that water—she could almost hear her singing as she scrubbed her one-and-only dress on the washboard.

Meggie brushed some stray tears off her cheeks, knowing that nothing would ever be the same for her again. *When I get back to Trout Lake and start eating my broccoli and offer to help*

Mom with the laundry, she's going to flat out faint. The trace of a smile began to move up one side of her tear-streaked face. Yeah. She knew things were going to be a lot different from now on.

"Meggie!" Paige yelled, breaking into her thoughts.

She whirled around, nearly dropping the diary.

"Oh, Meggie, I found something! You'll never believe it. Never!"

Anna's Treasures

Chapter 16

Meggie held the diary close and made her way across the shambles, stepping carefully over the rotting boards and fragments of furniture and rusted metal. She stepped off what might have once been the back porch, staring at her friend who was pulling some boards aside.

"Paige, what're you doing?"

"Look, Meggie!" Paige choked, pointing at the small white flowers that had been struggling upward towards the light.

"Oh, my gosh!" Meggie exploded, nearly dropping the diary. "Daisies! Oh, Paige! This *was* Anna's house! This was her backyard. Her garden! Meggie felt the words rushing like the swift, happy little creek where they had just found her treasures.

Paige nodded, her dark eyes filling with the same happy tears. "I know! Not even the cold winters killed her daisies. It's a miracle."

"Hello there!" a familiar voice called out, breaking into their celebration. "Johnny told me what happened."

Meggie turned and saw Johnny and his sister coming toward them. Ranger Downing had Anna's tin box in her hands. Meggie stood by the daisies and held the diary close to her pounding heart. It was time to give it up now, wasn't it? They would have to say goodbye to Anna and everything that was hers. They would even have to say goodbye to these little daisies blooming right through the boards and junk at their feet. *Oh, Anna...*

"You've made a wonderful discovery," Ranger Downing told them. "Johnny told me everything—including how the diary almost jumped up from the floor boards into your hands." A twinkle in her grey-green eyes told Meggie they weren't in trouble. "Next time, though, call us and report what you've found," Ranger Downing said. "We need to keep Bodie just as we've found it—in its state of arrested decay. If people begin moving things and digging around without special permission, that won't happen."

Meggie swallowed hard.

"By the way, Johnny also told me about the gun shots up near Rough Creek."

"Oh yeah..." Paige almost fell backwards over some boards.

"Probably old Mr. Lynch and his wife Jane," she told them. "They scare off anybody and everybody who strays onto their land. Just hitting clouds, though," she added. "They're really quite harmless."

Meggie felt better. A lot better.

"This has been a wonderful discovery, though, and we'll see that this girl's diary and treasures are kept in the Museum. Johnny says you found her treasures sealed in a rock up at Rough Creek," she went on. "My guess is that the rock contained some copper ore. Copper preserves almost anything it touches."

Meggie thought of the battered tin that held Anna's diary. That was copper too, wasn't it? No wonder it had been kept so safe for all those years. Meggie shook her head, amazed at the way everything seemed to be turning out.

"Do you realize you're going to be sharing her treasures with hundreds—even thousands of people?" Ranger Downing told her and Paige.

Meggie nodded, feeling Anna's words rushing like the tears that wanted to come. ...*Of course God could help himself to the dough balls or share my treasures with anyone he chooses...*

"Can you put her treasures and this diary next to her picture?" Paige asked, her wide brown eyes holding Ranger Downing's gaze.

"Her picture?"

Paige nodded. "In the Museum there's a picture of girl who's just about our age. She's holding some daisies."

"Oh yes. That lovely child in the display case. Johnny showed me. She's beautiful, isn't she? But we don't know who she is," Ranger Downing told Meggie and Paige. "She's an unknown girl from Bodie."

"We know who she is," Paige said, leaning down and pointing to the small white daisies reaching for the sun. "If you read her diary, you'll learn about her garden. You'll learn about these daisies she planted right here. Her name is Anna and she's holding some daisies just like these in that picture." Paige's words came slow and deliberate, trembling slightly like the small brave flowers at her feet.

Meggie's eyes blurred, amazed that the little daisies were still blooming after all these years. *You're still here in a way, aren't you, Anna? Blooming. Smiling up at the sun year after year. Smiling up at us this very minute...*

Ranger Downing gazed down at the daisies and then looked around at the remains of the old house. "I'll check it out," she said to the girls. "I promise. You may be right."

"I know we are," Meggie told her, hearing her heart beat against the old leather book she held so close. "She's Anna. Anna Louise Lockmoor. She came to Bodie in 1879."

"Let's take these things back to the Museum and put them in the display case, and then I'll give you the tin," Ranger Downing said.

Johnny beamed.

"Give us the what?" Meggie looked at Ranger Downing and then at Johnny who were both smiling.

"The park rangers here at Bodie want you to keep Anna's tin," Johnny said, his dust-streaked face smiling with pleasure. "If it wasn't for you two finding the diary and all, her treasures would still be stuck in that rock up at Rough Creek. Now her treasures will be here at Bodie so that everyone's gonna remember her."

Meggie's heart soared. "You mean we get to keep her little box?"

Johnny and his sister nodded.

Paige was so happy, she started jumping, dust and boards flying.

"Be careful, Paige!" Meggie laughed, clinging to the diary and Ranger Downing's words. They didn't want to make the park service mad and mess up. Not now. Everything was turning out better than she'd dreamed.

They walked back toward the Museum so that they could empty the treasures from Anna's tin. Paige asked to carry it, opening it slowly and gazing at Anna's treasures one last time.

"Wait a minute," Paige said, stopping in her tracks.

Meggie paused. "What's wrong, Paige?"

"Why didn't I think of it? It's not here. It's not here, Meggie!"

"What's not here?

"The locket. Anna's locket!"

Meggie caught her breath, realizing Paige was right. Johnny Merritt had taken Anna's locket. Just like she wanted him to! Anna's words returned: *I'll give him my locket with my picture inside. He won't hanker to wear it of course, but if anything happens to me, he can always keep my picture and remember me. Yes, when he comes tomorrow, I'll tell him he must fetch it from my tin of treasures and keep it for always and ever.*

Suddenly Meggie's heart fell. *If anything happens to me, he can keep my picture and remember me...If anything happens to me...If anything happens to me...* Meggie threw her hand over her mouth. Then something did happen, didn't it? *Oh, no. No, Anna.*

"A locket?" It was Ranger Downing now. She stood against the shadows of the late afternoon sun, brushing her soft hair from her questioning face.

"In her diary, Anna told her friend Johnny that he could keep her locket with her picture," Paige told her. "And since it's not here, we know he took it. She wanted him to."

"John—Johnny?" Ranger Downing moved closer.

"Johnny Merritt," Paige told her.

Ranger Downing's chin fell and she threw her hand over her

mouth, stunned. "What?"

"We have a grandpa named John Merritt," Johnny put in, turning to Meggie and Paige. "I wanted to say something, but I didn't think..."

Meggie gasped. "Whaaa...?"

Still overcome, Ranger Downing could scarcely speak. "Our grandfather, John—Johnny Merritt was named after his great grandfather who grew up in Bodie," Ranger Downing said, her eyes welling up.

"Johnny Merritt was your—your great-great..." Meggie couldn't finish. This was too awesome. Unreal.

"Grandma Merritt has the locket," Ranger Downing went on, the tears coming freely now. "I've never seen it, but Johnny or I will have it someday. Just like the name 'Johnny,' the locket has been passed down through the Merritt family for generations. Now I wish I'd asked Grandma to show me. She kept it in her trunk in the attic. She never wanted anything to happen to it."

"Anna's picture will be inside," Paige told her, wiping her tear-streaked face. "You'll know that's Anna in the Museum when you see the same picture in that locket."

Meggie turned away. She couldn't speak. But Johnny spoke. She listened to his words through the sounds of laughter and sadness filling her heart.

"I feel so proud," he said quietly. "I'll take care of her garden every year when I come to Bodie. I'll water Anna's daisies."

Chapter 17

After Meggie and Paige left Anna's diary at the Museum and said goodbye to Johnny and Ranger Downing, they paused and gazed across the decaying remains of Bodie to say one last goodbye.

They stood in silence, knowing this was one ghost town they would never forget.

"We'll take turns keeping her tin box, okay, Paige?"

Paige tossed her hair out of her wide eyes and nodded.

"What're you gonna keep in it when it's your turn?" Meggie asked.

"I'm not sure," Paige said quietly. "My most special things, I guess. What about you?"

A soft, hot wind blew Meggie's hair in circles as she opened the tin box with the small, faded flowers on top. "I don't know if I have anything as special as Anna had."

Paige was silent, then looked up into Meggie's face and smiled. "My dad sent me a gold necklace for my birthday and—and I wasn't even gonna keep it. But now..." her voice caught, "now maybe I—I'll put it in that box."

Meggie swallowed hard, but she couldn't say anything. Yet somehow, she knew she didn't have to. Paige's smile told her all she needed to know.

Anna had given them so much, hadn't she? Meggie's eyes filled as she clung to the little tin, thankful they had something to remember her by.

"I just wish we knew what happened to her though," Paige said.

And something did happen to her, didn't it? Meggie brushed a strand of hair from her moist eyes and nodded. "She told Johnny to take the necklace if something happened."

"I mean, everybody has to go sometime, Meggie. Even Anna. But I just wish we knew for sure that everything was okay for her. I keep thinking of her under that wool quilt with the cold winds coming through the cracks in her house..."

Meggie's heart felt heavy as she stroked the inner surface of the tin box absently. Yes, and would this feeling—this lead-weight feeling of never knowing ever go away? Then suddenly, she felt something odd beneath her hand. *Huh? What's this?* She caught her breath.

"What's wrong?" Paige asked.

Meggie's finger had caught a ridge at the bottom of the box and it was moving. "Paige..."

Paige edged closer. "Yeah?"

"Paige—there's something here..." Meggie's fingers trembled as she slowly slid a thin layer of tin—a false bottom—from the box. "Oh my gosh. I can't believe this." Her pulse raced as she pulled out a scrap of paper that had been folded carefully in its hiding place. Meggie held her breath and unfolded the fragile, yellowed thing that had been torn out of a book. A diary..

"Oh, Meggie!" Paige gasped. "Is that it? Is that the last page missing from her diary?"

Meggie and Paige stared at the words blurring before their eyes. The bright Bodie sun smiled down on Anna's final words. Her final gift.

Hello God, I'm leaving Bodie

POSTSCRIPT

Aunt Abby waved from the parking lot, motioning for them to come. Meggie slipped the last page of Anna's diary back into the tin box and held it close. It was time to leave the ghost town once known as the wildest town in the West.

"Looks like maybe God never did make it to Bodie," Paige said, her eyes as round and glazed as two dough balls.

Meggie paused, turning back one last time to say a silent goodbye to Bodie. And to Anna.

"Maybe not, Paige. But I think he sent an angel."